From
Charlie's
Point of
View

FROM CHARLIE'S
POINT OF VIEW

RICHARD SCRIMGER

SLEUTH
DUTTON

page vii: Lyrics for the R.E.M. song "Walk Unafraid" by Peter Buck, Mike Mills, and Michael Stipe. © 1998 Temporary Music (BMI). All rights on behalf of Temporary Music (BMI) administered by Warner-Tamerlane Publishing Corp. (BMI). All rights reserved.

DUTTON CHILDREN'S BOOKS
A division of Penguin Young Readers Group

Published by the Penguin Group • Penguin Group (USA) Inc., 375 Hudson Street, New York, New York 10014, U.S.A. • Penguin Group (Canada), 10 Alcorn Avenue, Toronto, Ontario, Canada M4V 3B2 (a division of Pearson Penguin Canada Inc.) • Penguin Books Ltd, 80 Strand, London WC2R 0RL, England • Penguin Ireland, 25 St Stephen's Green, Dublin 2, Ireland (a division of Penguin Books Ltd) • Penguin Group (Australia), 250 Camberwell Road, Camberwell, Victoria 3124, Australia (a division of Pearson Australia Group Pty Ltd) Penguin Books India Pvt Ltd, 11 Community Centre, Panchsheel Park, New Delhi–110 017, India • Penguin Group (NZ), Cnr Airborne and Rosedale Roads, • Albany, Auckland 1310, New Zealand (a division of Pearson New Zealand Ltd) • Penguin Books (South Africa) (Pty) Ltd, 24 Sturdee Avenue, Rosebank, Johannesburg 2196, South Africa
Penguin Books Ltd, Registered Offices: 80 Strand, London WC2R 0RL, England

Library of Congress Cataloging-in-Publication Data
Scrimger, Richard, date.
Charlie's point of view / by Richard Scrimger.—1st ed.
p.   cm.
Summary: Best friends Bernadette and Charlie begin seventh
grade and help unravel the mysterious case of the Stocking Bandit.
ISBN 0-525-47374-2
[1. People with disabilities—Fiction. 2. Blind—Fiction.
3. Best friends—Fiction. 4. Friendship—Fiction.
5. Mystery and detective stories.]   I. Title.
PZ7.S43617Ch   2005
[Fic]—dc22   2004011128

Published in the United States by Dutton Children's Books,
a division of Penguin Young Readers Group • 345 Hudson Street, New York, New York 10014
www.penguin.com/youngreaders

Designed by Irene Vandervoort   Printed in USA   First Edition
1   3   5   7   9   10   8   6   4   2

To faster horses, carrying more weight

ACKNOWLEDGMENTS

I would like to thank Sanjay Burman, who pushed me;
Scott Treimel, who talks as fast as I do, and more persuasively;
Maureen Sullivan in New York and Kathy Lowinger in Toronto, whose
enthusiasm and concern made it a much better manuscript;
Victoria Owen at the CNIB; and especially Gwen and
Elizabeth Holmes and Ben McConnell, who showed me
a small piece of their world. Thank you. Thank you.

I am happy to acknowledge the financial support of the
Canada Council for the Arts.

everyone walks the same
expecting me to step
the narrow path they've laid
they claim to
walk unafraid
I'll be clumsy instead
hold my love me or leave me
high

—MICHAEL STIPE

And, behold, the Lord passed by, and a great and strong wind rent the
mountains, and brake in pieces the rocks before the Lord; but the Lord was not
in the wind: and after the wind an earthquake; but the Lord was not in the
earthquake: and after the earthquake a fire; but the Lord was not in the fire: and
after the fire a still small voice.

—I KINGS 19:11—12

CONTENTS

CHAPTER ONE

CHAPTER TWO

CHAPTER THREE

CHAPTER FOUR

CHAPTER FIVE

**From
Charlie's
Point of
View**

CHAPTER ONE

SCENE 1: *Bernadette*

 Bernadette Lyall reaches out one skinny purple-pajama-covered arm to shut off her alarm clock. Now it is official. The school year has begun. While she was asleep, it was still summer, but now it is seven o'clock and a new term beckons. Actually, it doesn't beckon, it grabs her and drags her forward like a big dog on a leash.

New school: Schuyler Colfax Middle School. New teachers, new classmates. They'll have to take a bus to get there. Six stops. And the school is so big—you could fit the entire population of Kim Campbell Elementary into one of the new corridors. She hopes she'll be able to get the two of them from classroom to classroom without losing their way.

The two of them. Bernadette Lyall and Charles Fairmile. Bernie and Charlie. Inseparable since kindergarten. Of course he'd be lost without her, but she can't imagine school without him either. Bernadette sits up straight and pushes her hair off her face. There's a lot of it to push. Bernadette's hair is like whatever it is in that gospel song—*so high, you can't get over it, so wide you can't get around it.* Dark as night, and almost as scary. She slides out of bed without rumpling the covers. Her clothes are laid out from last night: black top, black pants, black socks. All her clothes are black, except her underwear. It is white. Mom doesn't believe in little girls wearing black underwear.

"It makes you look like a tramp," she said last month in the neighborhood discount store, a converted movie theater down the block from their apartment building.

Bernadette hates that store. The aisles are sticky from thirty years of chewing gum and spilled soda. Fat moms paw through ripped plastic bags and yell at their children, who ignore them. The smell of chemical disinfectant mixes with old popcorn and cigarette smoke. They have shopped there as long as Bernadette can remember.

"Aw, Mom," she said. "No one will see it."

"Says you."

"And anyway, *you* wear black underwear, Mom."

"So?"

Bernadette stares at herself in the cracked bathroom mirror: skin and bones and freckles, a button nose, and hair that won't stay combed. Oh, well.

Strangely, Mom is up early and, even more strangely, in a good mood. Wrapped in a rainbow-colored robe, she leans back against the counter. Coffee cup at her elbow, cigarette in her mouth. Dreamy look in her eyes.

"Hey there, hon! How are you this morning? Grab yourself some cereal. There's Froot Loops. Let me get out of your way so you can sit down. I mean, how the hell are you?" The cigarette bobs jauntily in her mouth when Cherie Lyall speaks. Bernadette is careful to keep her hair away from the lit end—not an easy task in a kitchen the size of a Volkswagen Beetle.

"Um, fine."

"Great. That's great." Cherie chuckles. "Just great. Have some cereal."

"Mom, how many of your pills have you had?"

She laughs so hard she starts to cough. Bernadette pours herself some cereal. Mom finishes coughing and spits into the pitted metal sink. "Don't make me laugh when I'm inhaling," she says.

"Sorry."

"No pills, you little monkey. I'm feeling too good. I had a

wonderful sleep. Did you have a wonderful sleep? How are you this morning? Oh, yeah, you told me. Fine. Sheeh, I'm better than fine. I woke up with the biggest smile on my face, I tell you. See, I had this dream."

Bernadette has overheard her mom describing dreams to friends. They often involve soap-opera stars. "Mom, I don't need to—"

"It was about your father." Cherie smiles broadly, remembering all over again. "I was killing him, the little rattlesnake. With my bare hands."

The apartment door, four years ago. Afternoon. Sun shining through the living-room window, making a diamond pattern on the floor. A wiry little man with greasy hair and scarred knuckles from a fight. "Well, bye," he says.

"Bye, Dad."

"I'll see you, sometime."

"Uh-huh."

"Get the hell out of here, Gary, ya bum!" Mom called from the living room.

The divorce never came through. Bernadette's parents are still married. There isn't a day she didn't think of it.

Sun's around the other side of the apartment building this morning. The kitchen window faces west. Bernadette checks the best-before date before pouring the milk. Her mom notices.

"Honestly, honey, you are a picky one. You're like what's-her-name's daughter. You know her, the cashier at the Money Mart. She has a daughter, thirteen, like you, and—Edna, that's her name. Not the daughter, the cashier. Her daughter's name is Anastasia, and she actually checks the due date on cough syrup! Would you believe it? And Tylenol. We had a good laugh about that."

Bernadette spoons Froot Loops into her mouth. Her mom butts out the cigarette and goes over to pour herself another cup of coffee.

"Yes, it was a great dream. There he was on his knees, Gary Lyall, my lawfully wedded husband, with his head tilted back, and my hands around his neck. You know how you can do anything in a dream? Fly, even? Well, I could keep your father down on his knees, and I stood over him with my hands around his neck, and I was squeezing like a son of a gun, and—"

"Mom. Please."

"What? It's not real, honey. It's a dream. Don't go thinking I'd kill anyone in real life. I'm too gentle. I revere life. I heard a woman say that on TV. 'I revere life,' she said, looking up to heaven. A gospel singer, big as a whale, but with the voice of an angel. I feel just like her. I revere life. I couldn't kill." She slurps coffee. "Though if I *was* going to kill anyone, it'd be your father. His eyes'd bug out, like they did in the dream. And then I'd—"

"Mom, I'm eating here."

Speaking of which, there's something funny about the Froot Loops. They should have gone soggy by now, but something in her mouth is crunching. Bernadette opens the cereal box and stares inside.

"Aw, Mom. Look! There's things with legs in here. In my bowl, too."

"How many of 'em?"

"I don't know. Lots. Ew." She feels around the inside of her mouth with her tongue.

"No, hon, I meant how many legs? Six legs . . . eight legs . . . a million legs?"

Her mouth seems clean. Bernadette pokes around the bowl with her spoon. Floating black things. Why didn't she notice? "They're insects, Mom. Six legs, I guess. One, two, three, four . . . I only see four legs." She swallows. "Geesh, I wonder if I could have . . ."

Her mom gazes out the window, a dreamy look still on her face, smoke spiraling up into the air. Not paying a lot of attention. "Four legs. Hmm. Deer have four legs. And they travel in herds, don't they? I saw a news special about deer in cities. They're in big parks, and sometimes they wander out into the streets. They can be a real hazard to traffic."

Bernadette frowns at her mother. What can you do? It's like Mom's head is a big house filled with different rooms. Sometimes she gets lost in there. She was a pretty girl. There's a framed picture on her dresser—Mom and some long-haired guy at an amusement park. She's eighteen or nineteen, wearing a polka-dot top and blue jeans, and smiling. Sometimes Bernadette wonders what happened to the pretty girl in the picture.

Mom sighs now and scratches herself. The synthetic material of the rainbow-colored bathrobe rustles. "Funny, I'd have thought we were too far downtown for deer."

Bernadette pushes away her cereal bowl. "I think I'll brush my teeth and go get Charlie."

SCENE 2: *Charlie*

Charlie's kitchen is just down the hall from Bernadette's, and unlike hers, it is warm and welcoming. And, as far as he can tell, spotless. The counters are clean under his fingers; the floor is freshly polished so that his socks glide over it. The smells are toast and butter, eggs, coffee, and lemon-scented dish soap. The sounds, apart from his fork scraping along the edge of the plate and his mother breathing, are a string quartet on the radio. Charlie's plate is almost empty now, but his stomach is full of nourishing scrambled eggs, fresh orange juice, toast, and a fruit-flavored pill containing his daily vitamin requirements, plus iron and folic acid.

In short, the small room reeks with love and care.

Charlie's mother stands behind him. Gladys Fairmile is a slight, angular woman. Caring mother, committed social worker, devoted wife, she gives off a sense of goodness stretched thin. Not much fat on her body or in her schedule. Charlie loves her, knows he needs her, but wishes she was easier to be with.

He can feel her warm breath on the back of his neck. He can feel her gaze: tender, dedicated, intense. He doesn't like it, but he's used to it. Good thing his dad is around to lighten Mom up. Briefly, Charlie wonders what life would be like without Dad. He shivers.

His mom notices, of course. "Are you cold, Charlie?" she asks, putting her hand on his shoulder.

"Huh? Oh, no. Just...uh...thinking of something."

"Do you want a sweater?"

"No. No, thanks, Mom. It's actually pretty warm. A nice day."

"How are the eggs, this morning, Charlie?" she asks. "Too dry?"

"No, they're fine."

"What about the toast? I put out an extra slice for you."

"Perfect."

"Your father's eggs will be dry by the time he gets here, if he doesn't hurry up. He's been ages getting dressed."

Charlie finishes his juice. He can't decide if he's finished breakfast or not. Maybe one more bite of toast.

"You're wearing the dark outfit today," his mom says.

Is she talking to him? Dad has a dark outfit, too. Charlie turns around in his chair.

"Charlie, did you hear me? I said you're wearing the dark outfit today."

"Am I?"

"It looks nice. The stripes in the shirt are very tasteful. You know, they're the same color as the frames of your sunglasses."

"Uh-huh." He doesn't care in the least.

"Gladys!"

His father's comfortable baritone climbs alarmingly up the scale. "Gladys, come here and look at this! I've got holes in every one of my black socks."

Charlie's mother sighs. "Oh, Roger. Are you sure, dear? I just bought you some more black socks last week."

Charlie hears a clatter by the sink and his mother's footsteps fading as she leaves the kitchen. Is he finished? Did his mother clear his dishes? He reaches out cautiously. His father's plate is there, but Charlie's placemat, still warm from the plate, is empty.

"I guess I'm finished," he says.

Charlie's point of view depends mostly on hearing, touch, smell, and imagination. What he actually sees of the world is:

Charlie is blind. Stone blind, bottom-of-a-midnight-well blind. He has been from birth. It doesn't really bother him. How could it? He doesn't know what he's missing, any more than you know what it's like to be telepathic. No, you don't.

He reaches for his napkin. He folds the unused paper square in half to make a triangle, then folds two sides of the triangle toward the middle. He hears his parents talking. Dad is running late. Mom is sympathetic. She always is. Charlie folds the napkin three more times, producing a slightly lopsided crane.

Roger Fairmile enters the room. "Son, I'm sorry." What's that smell? Charlie wrinkles his nose.

"That's okay, Dad."

"You don't even know what I'm apologizing for."

"Your cologne?"

"Don't be smart, Charlie. I'm late for work. It's already . . ."

"Eight-fourteen," says Charlie.

"And I'm nowhere ready to leave. First I cut myself shaving. Then I broke a belt loop, so I had to change into yesterday's pants, and then I spilled cologne all over. And now I can't find any black socks without holes. My morning is a mess. And I've got an early meeting about security. I'm going to have to take a cab to make it on time."

Charlie's dad works in a bank. He is an assistant to the assistant branch manager. He's not supposed to wear the same suit two days in a row. It's company policy.

"That's okay, Dad. Bernadette and I will take the bus by ourselves."

"That's what I'm getting at. Do you think you can?"

"Of course," says Charlie. "We've practiced. We know the route. We've lived in the city all our lives. And we're fourteen years old, you know. We're not kids."

"I wanted to meet your teacher. He's supposed to be very good. Very innovative."

"You can meet him some other time, Dad."

"I suppose so."

"Are you sure you'll be okay?" asks his mom. "Are you sure, Charlie?" She works in a day care. She spends a lot of time asking people if they are sure.

"Sure I'm sure."

"Well, if you're sure. You will be there to pick him up, Roger? Won't you?"

"Hmm-hmmm," says Dad with his mouth full. "I'm sure, too."

"That's good." She approaches, sniffing the air. "Are you really wearing . . . cologne, Roger?" she asks, in a suddenly husky voice. "You don't usually."

"They were giving out samples at the bank yesterday. Some kind of promotion. I wanted to surprise you."

"I'm surprised, all right," says Charlie.

"No, not you. Do *you* like it, Gladys, my aproned angel?"

"Oh, my financial turtledove, I do. I know you're late, but I can't resist that smell." She inhales deeply. "Mmm, I do like it. Very musky."

"Mmm."

They kiss deeply, noisily. Charlie shakes his head. "You know, there are times when I'm really glad I'm blind."

"Mmm. Kiss me again, you fiduciary Adonis," says Gladys.

"I love it when you talk that way."

The couple continue to kiss passionately behind Charlie, who is, for now, forgotten. The traffic noise rises from the street below. The clock ticks. Their sighs deepen.

The music starts up again. Something lively, with trumpets.

Charlie clears his throat. "You folks about done?"

They stumble, and bump against the table. The butter dish moves. His father swears.

Charlie hears Bernadette's special knock at the front door. "Time for me to go," he says. Crossing to the fridge, he takes his lunch from the regular shelf on the left, closes the fridge door, and walks steadily to the hall. He doesn't have to count paces at home—he knows the apartment better than you know your pocket—and yet he can't help noticing how many steps it is from the kitchen to the hall closet. Sixteen. At the beginning of the summer it was seventeen. He's grown again. He can remember when it was twenty paces. He can remember when it was more than he could count.

Roger hurries after him. Charlie hears his footsteps, then his voice. "Wait up, son."

He turns, points his face at his father.

"Let me help you get ready. Here's your backpack."

He holds it out for Charlie, who shrugs into the straps. "Thanks."

"And your white cane. Got your what-is-it—the braille computer?"

"My Louis Light? It's in the backpack, Dad."

"Oh, yeah. Pretty heavy."

"Yeah."

A small silence.

"I want you to know that I'm really proud of you, Charlie. With Bernadette around, you'll do just fine today. I know you will." He coughs, embarrassed.

"Thanks, Dad."

"You guys did great at the practice session. Right up until the end, that is."

"Yes."

"Now I've got to go and change my shirt. There's butter all down the sleeve. I'll see you after school, okay?"

"Okay, Dad."

"And, son, remember what I told you. When you get to the classroom, find a place you can hear."

Footsteps fade toward his parents' bedroom.

Scene 3: *Charlie and Bernadette*

"Hey there." He can hear the smile in Bernadette's voice.

"Hey yourself." Charlie strikes a man-of-adventure pose. "So, where do you want to go today?"

"Did somebody say 'seventh grade'?"

He chuckles. "There's a little seventh grade in everyone. Say, do you mind going on the bus by ourselves? Dad's running late."

"Can do."

Now Charlie smiles. *Can do* is one of Bernadette's favorite phrases. She is so competent. Charlie can't remember ever hearing her ask for help.

For her part, Bernadette is pleased—almost relieved—to be in charge. She'd rather not have to depend on someone else. Anyone else. Charlie's parents are nice, but . . . well, they're parents. How far can you really trust them?

Now here's his mom, looking worried.

"Good morning, Bernadette. I'm sorry Roger can't go

with you and Charlie this morning. Are you sure you can get yourselves to school?"

"I'm sure, Mrs. Fairmile." She's used to Charlie's mom. Gives her the bright-smile-for-adults.

"Good. How are you feeling, this morning? And how's your mom?"

"Fine, Mrs. Fairmile. Mom is feeling great this morning."

"The bus will be at our stop any minute," says Charlie. "Bye, Mom." He raises his voice. "Bye, Dad!"

Bernadette hears an inarticulate bellow from somewhere in the apartment. Mrs. Fairmile says, "Oh, dear," and runs off.

Bernadette leads, with Charlie hanging on to her elbow. That way, he just does what she does. If she has to stop, or climb upstairs, he knows to do it, too.

The elevator bumps to a noisy stop, and lets them on. "Careful," says Bernadette. "Small step down."

The two ladies inside the elevator smile over their laundry baskets and go on with their conversation. The older one, a white-haired knitter named Miss Callaghan (no one knows her first name), is talking.

"I saw her at the Mini-Mart yesterday, Desiree. I was behind her in line. Her wallet was stuffed with twenties."

"Is that a fact?" Desiree Danton (hardly anyone uses her last name) is a blowsy brunette with a two-packs-a-day voice.

"Every time I see her she's got a new ring, or coat. Not something you'd get at the circus, either. Something expensive! I tell you I don't know why she stays in this dump."

They sigh.

"Good morning, Desiree. Morning, Miss Callaghan," says Charlie. Their voices are easy to recognize.

"Hey, Charlie. Hey, Bernadette," says Desiree.

"Hello, children." Miss Callaghan raises her eyebrows at Bernadette. "How's your mother this morning, dear? I thought she was a bit . . . tired when I saw her last night."

Tired. She means drunk. "Well, she's not tired now, Miss Callaghan."

The elevator descends slowly, like an old cat coming downstairs. The ladies nudge each other. Miss Callaghan clears her throat. "Do you . . . happen to have the time, Charlie?" she asks.

"I always have the time, Miss Callaghan," says Charlie. "It's eight twenty-one."

Bernadette sighs and looks away. The same old routine every time they meet. How can Charlie put up with people treating him like a freak?

Miss Callaghan shivers with pleasure. "Amazing!" she says.

"It's just a knack," says Charlie. The elevator stumbles to a stop. "Good-bye, ladies. Have a nice day."

"Level floor," says Bernadette, and the two of them get off.

"He's so polite," whispers Miss Callaghan as the elevator descends to the basement. "None of that teenage attitude."

"And so handsome. You'd never suspect anything was wrong with him. If it weren't for the white cane and the sunglasses, you'd swear he was just like anyone else."

"Bernadette—now, she's got an attitude. Did you notice her rolling her eyes?"

"Oh, yes."

"I'd slap her silly if she was mine," says Miss Callaghan.

The morning is bright and warm, with a high sky. Somehow it is definably not summer. A hint of coolth, a hint of regret, whatever it is that signifies the first day of school. Bernadette gives Charlie her elbow and leads him out the front door. Across Copernicus Street, the oldest cemetery in the city stretches the length of the block and away into the distance. Sun glints off the spikes of the high metal fence.

Bernadette likes it that her bedroom overlooks the cemetery. Sometimes, when her mom is yelling into the phone or at the TV, Bernadette will go to her bedroom and just stare out at the quiet trees and stones.

"Say, Charlie, do you guys have pests in your apartment?" she asks. "This morning I found things crawling in my cereal. Horrible things with legs. Careful." She guides him around a fire hydrant and trips over a panhandler sitting cross-legged on the sidewalk. "Sorry, Uriah," she says.

"S'okay, Bernadette," says the panhandler.

"I had eggs for breakfast," says Charlie.

The city bus pulls up slowly. Bernadette hustles Charlie to the head of the bus line, her little elbows working like pistons. "Coming through," she cries. "Excuse me there, excuse us. Thank you. Stairs now, Charlie." He hangs on to her elbow, climbing into the bus easily.

"Hey there, Bernadette. Hey, Charlie," wheezes the bus driver, a fat man in a short-sleeved shirt.

"Hey, Alf," says Charlie. "You're two and a half minutes late this morning."

"I know." Alf takes their tickets quickly, jerkily. He does everything like that. "Accident on Dundas Street, two idiots yelling in the middle of the road. Traffic's backed up for blocks. *Step right up there!* And my big toe's killing me."

Bernadette finds them seats together at the back of the bus. The vehicle fills up and starts off in a series of belches and jerks. Bernadette peers past Charlie out the window. "Hey, there's Mrs. Yodelschmidt, from the ninth floor. She's the one the nasty old ladies on the elevator were talking about."

"Mrs. Yodelschmidt—she has a dog, right?"

"Yup. A poodle named Casey. He's with her now."

"Do you think she really is rich?"

Bernadette considers. "She didn't used to be. Last winter she shopped at the dented-can store. Now she's wearing a fur coat."

"In September?"

"And a matching hat. Yes, I think she's rich now."

"Rich and warm."

The bus hurls itself forward and stops like a hockey player hitting the boards. Bernadette catches herself in time. She mutters under her breath.

"You nervous?" asks Charlie.

"About what? First day at a brand-new school? New kids, new teachers? And worried about you all the time? Nah."

He nods. Not quite at her, but close. "Me neither."

"Besides, we know our way around Schuyler Colfax now." Bernadette starts to laugh.

"Thinking about the O and M?" He laughs himself, even though he was on the bottom of the pile.

O and M stand for *Orientation* and *Mobility.* The idea was for Charlie to get used to Schuyler Colfax School. How many paces from the sidewalk to the front door? How many stairs to the second floor? Which way did the doors open? How far from their homeroom to the cafeteria; to his educational assistant's office; to the bathroom? They took it in stages, hallway by hallway. Bernadette led Charlie, and then they went back and he did it on his own. It was a July afternoon, ripe for a thunderstorm and hot enough to raise tar bubbles on the playground. The principal kept apologizing. Charlie's new EA, Titus Underglow III, a society do-gooder who pronounced *Charles* to rhyme with *falls,* was sweating so hard he kept dropping his gold-handled umbrella.

Charlie did well, tapping forward confidently. Bernadette expected him to crash into a wall when two hallways intersected, but he never did. He always stopped, and then turned correctly. "How do you know when you come to an intersection?" she asked.

"The cane sounds different," he explained. "The sound isn't bouncing off a wall anymore—there's a hallway stretching away from me. And I can feel wind on my cheek. It comes from a different place when a new hallway opens up."

Afterward, the principal, Mrs. Vox, wanted a photograph for the school newsletter. She posed them all in the main lobby, set the camera on a stand, and hurried into the picture herself. Unfortunately, at just that moment Charlie's white cane got tangled up with Mr. Underglow's umbrella. They fell together. On his way down, Charlie grabbed Bernadette, who clutched at Charlie's mom for support, who was clinging to Charlie's dad, who had his hand on the principal's shoulder. They all went down like grain stalks before a combine harvester, and the seven-hundred-dollar digital camera ended up in almost as many pieces on the stone floor.

"Do you remember all that stuff you learned at the O and M?" she asks now. "Forty-nine paces from the front door to the stairs and all that?"

He thinks back. He can feel the smooth stone floor of the school in his memory, hear the echo of his own voice in the halls, and Bernadette's. And the principal's, moaning about her camera. He can feel the door handles, positioned higher than his old school's, and smell the leftover food in the cafeteria. The bathroom was . . . where was it?

"Not all of it," he says. "I figure if I get lost, I'll ask someone."

"I'll be there."

"Then I'll ask you." He smiles in her direction.

"Charlie, does it bother you, depending on people? I'd hate it."

The bus jerks forward, but he's ready for it, braced against the window, feet firmly on the floor. The person ahead of him lets out a grunt of surprise.

"The way I see it, Bernie, everyone depends on someone. How would you like to have to survive without your mom?"

Silence.

"Sorry," he says. "Bad example. But look at it this way: We're depending on Alf right now to get us to school. He's depending on the people who fill the bus with gas and put up the road signs and traffic lights. They're depending on the people who write the traffic-flow programs for the computers. And *they're* depending on the people who make the microchips. And they are *all* depending on the schools to turn out students who know what they're doing. Which is us." He deepens his voice, trying for James Earl Jones. "So you see, Simba, we are all part of the great circle of—"

And, suddenly, Alf notices the kid at the crosswalk. He stamps on the brake pedal hard enough to threaten the hematoma on his right big toe. (A few more stops like that and the blood-filled sac is going to burst.) The bus screeches to a skidding halt just before the double white lines of the crosswalk. Horns blare. Charlie hears a cry from the seat next to him.

"Bernadette? Bernadette? You okay?" He feels around. The seat is empty. Surely she was sitting beside him just a moment ago.

"Back off, Grandpa!" She has been thrown into the aisle and trampled by standees nearby. She pushes an older man out of the way and climbs back into her seat. "No problem, Charlie," she says, slapping dust from her pants and shirt.

The bus starts off again.

"Where are we now? What else can you see out the window?" asks Charlie.

"Hmm." She peers past him. The bus turns a corner, honks, barrels forward, and stops again. "We're on Grant Street, by the Safeway and your dad's bank. An old lady is washing the sidewalk in front of her fruit store. A man is eating ice cream out of the carton. And—look, there's someone in a stocking mask running out of the bank!"

The bus accelerates past the scene. She stares backward. Is it real, or are they shooting a film? There have been a dozen bank-machine robberies this summer by a guy in a stocking mask. Always in the morning, come to think of it.

"You're kidding, right? About the mask? Is it that guy the police are after?"

"The Stocking Bandit? I don't know. Maybe." The robber, if it is a robber, is wearing a dark suit and carrying a bag or case. He runs down a side street. She can't see any cameras. No one shouts *"Cut!"*

"Maybe?"

The bus keeps going. The man disappears. The incident is over. Bernadette tries to re-create the picture in her mind. She can't. Did it really happen? Was it a dream?

"I don't know, Charlie."

"You mean, maybe it was really a woman in stockings?"

"I don't think so."

"And running?"

Bernadette laughs. "I don't know. Maybe she had a run in her stockings."

"I'm getting confused," says Charlie. He hears a siren coming toward them. Police or ambulance? Are they going to the scene of the crime? Is there really a bank robbery? What is going on? Deciding that he does not need to know, he settles back against the bus seat and waits for his stop. Day before yesterday, on the dry run, he and Bernadette reached the front of the school at exactly 8:36. It's almost that now.

When Bernadette touches his arm, he stands quickly. "Come on, let's go," she calls in a loud voice. "Out of the way, people. Coming through!" Bernadette clears a path for Charlie, elbowing other bus passengers out of the way. "What are you staring at?" she demands of an older lady with lots of makeup and an umbrella.

"A rude little girl," the old lady replies evenly.

"I apologize for my companion, madam," says Charlie over his shoulder. "She's having a difficult childhood."

"Hey!" Bernadette grabs Charlie hard. "You watch it."

"I wish I could," he says. An old joke between them.

"Oh, very funny."

The older lady stares after the two of them, shaking her head.

"Bye, Alf!" calls Bernadette, pulling Charlie down the bus steps after her.

Schuyler Colfax Middle School is set well back from the road, with a perimeter fence around a big asphalt playground. The school building itself is a forbidding block of gray concrete. It doesn't just sit there in the middle of the playground, it looms. The first time she saw it, Bernadette thought it was a prison.

She approaches the gate cautiously. There are so many strange kids! She knew every single person in her elementary school last year. Looking anxiously around her, she does not recognize a soul.

Charlie slouches along, seeming as calm as usual. Does he know kids are looking at him? Does he know there's a trio of high-school-aged skateboarders pumping down the sidewalk toward them?

No he doesn't. Bernadette pulls him to the curb so that the boarders can glide majestically past—or as majestically as you can glide with your boxer shorts showing and your mouth full of gum.

"Are you counting steps from the bus stop, Charlie?"

"No, just thinking."

"We're coming up to the school gate now." She leads him forward. Charlie cocks his head, listening to the sounds of the playground. Yelling, mostly. "I wonder if the people here will be nice."

At this point a kid named Frank Sponagle steers a bike right at them. He's way too big for the bike; its tires are flat to the ground. He stands up to pedal, laughing meanly as he approaches: "Haw haw haw!"

Bernadette sees him just in time. Her mind registers the striped shirt, the shaved head, the danger. She pushes Charlie through the gate into the playground and ducks behind a lamppost. Frank sprays saliva as he pedals past.

Bernadette winces, wipes her arm. "I wonder about that, too," she says.

"Hey, Bernie!" Charlie has his head cocked. "Listen! Do you hear?"

"What?"

"Music. Like a church choir. Can you hear it?"

"No."

Bernadette stands outside the gate, watching the striped-shirted bike rider. Something small and colorful flies through the air and hits his front wheel, knocking it sideways. The bike wobbles and falls over, bringing the oversized rider down with it. He lets out a yell. The small and colorful thing bounces along the sidewalk toward her. It's a hard rubber ball, not much bigger than a quarter, the kind of ball little kids get in birthday grab bags. It must have knocked against the spokes, bringing down the bike.

Where'd the ball come from? A passing car? And was the biker a chosen target or accidental victim? She looks up and down Grant Street, but can't find any answers to her questions.

"There. The music is gone now," says Charlie.

Bernadette picks up the ball. Mostly green with yellow stripes. Spring colors, she thinks. Colors of hope. She puts the ball in her pocket. "Church music, you said. Like a hymn?"

She doesn't doubt him. She's known Charlie almost all her life. He hates to be called special, but he is. Not special to be pitied—special because he really does seem to be in touch with something that she can't always recognize.

Actually, the word he likes to use for himself is handicapped. The way a horse is handicapped, he says, to make the race fair. It carries more weight because it's a faster horse. And remember, he says, there are lots of people out there carrying more weight than I am.

Whichever way you think about him, if Charlie heard church music, it was there.

"Not a hymn," he says. "More serious. More scary."

Schuyler Colfax Middle School is on a corner. Grant Street, the bus route, runs east and west. There's a smaller street running north and south. Across this street are a few low-rise brick apartment buildings with dirty narrow alleyways between them. The bricks were white once. Now they're gray. Bernadette's attention is distracted by noise and movement in one of the alleyways.

Action

"Oh, Charlie! There's a kid in trouble across the street."

"So?"

"A dog has him cornered."

"So?"

Bernadette peers anxiously across. At the back of the alleyway is a rickety wooden fence, with a pile of refuse and trash cans. Perched atop one can, menaced by a huge dog, is Lewis Ellieff, a short kid with curly dark hair and wire-rimmed glasses. A soft chubby kid with pink skin and a pale blue button-down shirt.

Not an attractive kid.

"Help!" he shouts. "Somebody, help! Anybody help! I'm in trouble here, and I really need someone to come to my assistance! Mad dog alert!"

Bernadette doesn't hesitate. "Come on, Charlie. We have to help him."

"Do we? Why?"

"He's smaller than we are, and he's in trouble."

Charlie frowns. "Is the dog smaller than we are?" Bernadette grabs his hand, places it on her elbow. "Step down," she says, and pulls him into traffic. "Hang on, kid!" she cries.

"Yes," calls Charlie, "hang on, kid! We're coming! Not that we have the faintest idea how to help you!" He admires the way Bernadette can throw herself into someone else's life. His own would be so much more difficult without her. But there are times when the ability to not see can make things easier.

"I have a plan," she says. "You distract the dog, Charlie, and I'll rescue the kid. You can keep the dog at bay with your cane."

He sighs. "That sounds like a good plan. After you rescue him, the two of you can rescue me."

Lewis is still calling. "Help, oh help! I'm going to die, I'm going to be eaten by a slavering monster who has bad breath because he's used to eating garbage! I'm going to be bitten and savaged. I read *The Hound of the Baskervilles*. I saw a special on *60 Minutes* about crazed animal killers! No, it wasn't *60 Minutes*. It might have been *20/20*. Anyway, I know what happens when pets go bad. My corpse will be unrecognizable. My parents will be so upset! My life is flashing before my eyes. Good-bye, Ma. Good-bye, Pa. Your little Lewis is going to turn into dog chow. Oh the horror, the horror!"

Charlie frowns thoughtfully. "Mouthy little guy, isn't he?"

Bernadette urges him across the street. "Come on, Charlie. Step up on the curb, here. There isn't much time."

"Why do you say that?"

Charlie stops in the middle of the sidewalk, plants his stick and lifts his head to the heavens. "All my life I've heard that. Hurry, Charlie, you'll miss the bus. There isn't much time. Hurry, Charlie, you'll be late. Everyone always says that at important moments. There isn't much time. Why isn't there much time? Where does it go? Why isn't it there when we need it? Why can't there, just once, be a lot of time?"

Action

And, as if by magic, there suddenly is a lot of time. The streetscape fades slowly, giving way to a backyard in a wealthy suburb. The sun hangs low in the west of a perfectly clear, windless sky. In the middle distance are flower beds full of scent and color, and acres of thick, fresh-cut grass. In the foreground is an Olympic-sized swimming pool, surrounded by a deck of pleasingly smooth slate tile. Charlie, wearing a belted towelling robe, fresh from a swim, relaxes in a cushioned canvas chair reclined at exactly the right angle for comfort. In his hand is a tall, cool glass of chocolate milk. Behind him is an umbrella table. On it, a radio is playing quietly: one of those slow country songs that never seems to get to the point. In the background, bees buzz, birds twitter. It is, in short, the quintessence of a lazy summer afternoon. Bernadette strolls across the deck, yawning.

"Oh, Charlie," she says, "I think we ... might as well save the kid now."

"So soon? Let me finish my drink first."

"Sure, Charlie. There's time."

"How much time?"

"Plenty of time. All the time you need."

"Good."

He slurps the end of his drink, puts down the glass. "Ahhh." He climbs slowly to his feet, stretches like a cat. "I guess I'm ready now," he says. He picks up his white cane and strides forward into reality.

Traffic noise is steady from behind them. The dog barks loudly in front of them. The kid is still babbling hysterically. "Hurry, Charlie!" says Bernadette, pulling him forward.

"About ten more steps." She raises her voice. "Don't worry, kid! We're coming!"

Bernadette is worried herself. What has she got them into? This is one mean dog. Can Charlie hold it off? "Put up your cane, Charlie!" she cries. "Point it like a sword. I'm going to call the dog."

"Call it what?"

"Distract it, I mean. Get it away from the kid. Here, boy!" she cries. "Come here!"

Charlie sighs, and reverses his grip on his cane.

The dog isn't coming. Bernadette keeps yelling. "Hey, you stupid mutt! Over here! Yes, I'm talking to you, and I'm calling you stupid! Come on, you four-footed lummox!"

She picks up an empty can, flings it in the dog's direction.

Now it turns and notices them. What a monster! It looks like a small horse. A horse with sharp teeth. Is that foam around its mouth? Bernadette swallows.

Charlie holds his cane in his right hand. His left is raised over his head, so that he looks like a fencer. "Is this the right direction?" he asks. Thank goodness Charlie is always calm.

"A bit to the left. Hey, kid, get ready to jump down. Okay?"

"Here?" asks Charlie. "Bernadette, is this okay? Am I pointing in the right direction?"

The dog charges.

But Charlie is still facing in slightly the wrong direction, and of course when he turns, he sees...

Action

35

The dog's barking is loud and deep. It comes closer. Charlie points his cane. And then, over the noise of the dog and the kid and the street, he hears it.

Bernadette hears it, too. It's like Charlie described it: church music. A choir singing. She catches a word. *Behold.*

The dog has stopped barking. Its head is down. It's going to leap. She screams. The fat kid, still on top of his trash can, screams. And everything seems to move in slow motion.

A small round projectile hits the pile of trash near the top. A puff of dust billows out. The impact of the projectile starts a broken skateboard rolling down a sloping sheet of cardboard. The skateboard gathers speed, squeaking as it goes. Just as the dog leaps at the boy, it is distracted by the sound of the skateboard. The leap is curtailed, and the dog lands well short of its target—lands, in fact, neatly on the moving skateboard, which rolls past the children and onto the street. There is an immediate cacophony of horns, brakes, crumpling metal, and shattering glass. The dog leaps from the skateboard and takes off down the road at top speed, its tail between its legs.

Bernadette's attention is distracted for just a moment by a lone figure standing on the top of the rickety wooden fence. A stocky, broad-shouldered boy with crew-cut hair. He wears a dress vest over his shirt, and baggy shorts. She only sees him for a second, so it's hard for her to tell how old he is. He might be her age. When he drops out of sight behind the fence, the choir music ends.

"Wow!" she says.

Charlie stops waving his cane around. "I heard the music," he says. "I take it the crisis has passed."

"Um, yes."

"It's eleven minutes to nine. We have to be getting to school."

The dorky-looking little kid jumps off his trash can and comes running over. "Hey! Hey, you guys. How are you? Thanks! Thanks a lot. My name's Lewis, by the way. Lewis with a *w*, not like St. Louis. That was real nice of you to come and save me. I was in trouble all right. Did you see the teeth on that beast?"

"Yes," says Bernadette.

"No," says Charlie.

"They shouldn't allow animals to roam around wild like that. This city is getting scarier and scarier. We live in those big white apartment buildings down Grant Street. My ma didn't want to let me go to school by myself, even though it's only a couple of stops. My pa told her she was crazy. She told him he was pathetic. Then they started to fight." He shakes his head, as if to clear it. "You know, that dog chased me across the street and down the alley. I got off the bus and there it was. I didn't notice right away because I was thinking about candy bars. Ever do that? I was thinking about the really big kind of candy bars—the kind they sell to cure cancer or buy football uniforms. . . ."

Bernadette leads Charlie across the road. Lewis follows along, talking all the while. The accident is not serious. The front of a red minivan is stuck to the rear bumper of a big fat white car. The skateboard is crushed under the white car's front wheel. Two women are standing toe-to-toe, pointing at each other. Traffic crawls past. Horns honk.

Bernadette notices something colorful lying in the gutter on the far side of the road. She bends to pick it up. A hard rubber ball, not much bigger than a quarter, the kind little kids get in birthday grab bags.

SCENE 5: *Lewis*

". . . and I got to the end of the alley, and I didn't have any-where to go. I swear I thought I was gone, cross my heart, hope to die, buried alive in a cemetery after dark. Did you see that monster? Where do they breed them like that? With the claws and the teeth and the slavering and all . . . *Whoo-ee!* I'm going to have that nightmare tonight. Tomorrow, too, I think. Yep, I'd say it was a three-nightmare experience. You ever do that? Figure out how scary a thing is by the number of nightmares you're going to have about it?"

Charlie's fingers tighten on Bernadette's elbow. She knows what he means. Funny kid, Lewis. Hasn't stopped talking once.

"I remember my aunt Mary Lee dressed up in a monster costume for Halloween. I was feeling sick to my stomach from having eaten so many hot dogs, and I opened the bathroom door, and there she was, gluing a giant nose onto her face in my bathroom mirror." He shivers. "That was an eight-nightmare situation. *Whoo-ee!* Let's hurry. I hope I'm not going to be late. It makes such a bad impression on the teacher. Say, what grade are you guys in? Grade seven? You look like you'd be in grade seven. I live with my ma and pa and—hey, you're blind!"

He stares at Charlie. Waves his hand in front of Charlie's face. Turns to Bernadette. "He's blind, isn't he? Isn't he?"

There's a pause. "Why don't you ask him?" says Bernadette.

Lewis stares at Charlie, momentarily distracted from himself. But not for long. "That's great. I mean, I hardly noticed it because you move so natural, so, you know, like anyone else. I'm almost blind, too. Without my glasses I wouldn't see anything. Feel how thick they are."

Charlie shakes his head. "It's okay, I—"

"No, feel them. Here they are. Feel how thick." Lewis takes off his glasses and puts them in Charlie's hands. Bernadette has to fight back a laugh. "Feel those lenses. Thick. That gives us something in common."

"Yes," says Charlie, handing them back.

Bernadette frowns. "What do you mean, I look like I'm in grade seven?"

Lewis shrugs. "Nothing, I guess. I mean . . ."

"You mean I'm short? Is that it? 'Cause I'm taller than you are."

Charlie laughs. "We're both in grade seven," he says. "I'm Charlie, and she's Bernadette."

Lewis waves his hands and keeps talking. "Well, I'm in grade seven, too, so we've all got something in common. We should—hey, watch out!" A shadow flits across the sun. Lewis, always on the edge of anxiety, now falls over that edge into panic. He covers his head and dives to the side.

Charlie does not move. There is no point.

Bernadette squints upward, identifies the shadow. "Frisbee," she announces.

"Ah."

A pink plastic disk lands beside them, spinning on the pavement. Not too far away, a group of fashionable girls, mostly blond, in stylish clothes, mostly tight, are giggling. Bernadette disengages Charlie's hand from her elbow, picks up the Frisbee, and sends it skimming back toward the girls. Her throw sails wide. The girls giggle some more. Oh, well.

"Is Lewis gone?" asks Charlie.

"No. He's just getting up and dusting himself off."

"Did you *see* that?" says Lewis. "Darn thing nearly took my head off!" He raises his voice, aiming it at the giggling girls. "Watch it, over there! There are people walking in this playground, you know! Handicapped people! Blind people!"

Charlie sighs.

The girls giggle again.

Bernadette stares past the giggling girls. Her heart leaps, and lodges in her throat. Can that chubby figure in the staff parking lot be her father? It looks like him. A lot like him.

The figure takes something off his windshield and waves at some students. He's a teacher. Bernadette swallows. Of course her father wouldn't come. Of course not.

Charlie senses her confusion. "What's wrong?"

"Nothing." She clears her throat.

Lewis shakes his head. "Some people have no respect," he says. "So, you're Bernadette and Charlie, hey? *B* and *C*. That'll be easy to remember. So, what class are you in? Are you together? I guess you are, hey? I mean—so—what class are you in, anyway?"

"We're in 7F with Mr. Floyd," says Bernadette.

"Hey, so am I. Great! My mom was afraid I wouldn't know anyone, and now—"

The bell rings. Something wrong with the clapper, so that what emerges is a harsh croaking sound, like a raven. Lewis shudders. "Hear that? Spooky, hey?"

Lewis

"Five to nine," says Charlie. "What happens now, Bernadette? Do we line up?"

"No. People seem to be marching right into school. Come on." She leads him forward.

Lewis follows them, talking away busily. "But, seriously, isn't it great that we're in the same class? You guys save me from the mad dog—well, you don't actually save me, but you try to save me, and you're there when I am saved—and it turns out that we're all in the same class. We'll be like the Three Musketeers! How about that!"

"Or the Three Stooges," says Bernadette.

"All for one, and one for all!" Lewis makes a dramatic flourish with his right arm. He's wearing cuff links.

Bernadette does a passable Curly imitation: "Whoo whoo whoo." One skinny arm is bent over her head. With the other she leads Charlie into school.

SCENE 6: *Setting*

Their classroom is Room 24. Sixty-five paces from the pull doorway at the head of the main entrance staircase. The sign on the door says 7F—MR. FLOYD.

"Here we are," says Bernadette, leading Charlie inside.

They stand for a moment in the doorway, sounds of the corridor behind them.

She describes the classroom for him. "Desks in rows, blackboard, teacher's desk with stacks of notebooks and textbooks. Windows along one wall. Fluorescent lights overhead. Typical, except for one thing."

"What?"

"No teacher."

Lewis is hovering around them nervously. "I wonder where the bully is," he whispers. "Every year it's the same. I always end up sitting beside the bully."

"It's good to have some sense of continuity in your life," says Bernadette.

Charlie deepens his voice to resemble the rich, full-throated murmur of a television commentator. "And welcome, ladies and gentlemen, to this September's version of that popular school game show, *Spot the Bully.* Bernadette, would you please evaluate the candidates to us as we meet them for the first time. Viewers at home may want to get a piece of paper and pencil and jot down their own impressions."

She fights back a giggle, leads him forward slowly. The class is staring, but Charlie seems completely at ease.

Lewis is anxious. He doesn't know what to do right now. Charlie is drawing attention to them, and Lewis is very leery of other people's attention.

Bernadette leads Charlie along the front of the class. He grasps his white cane so that the top protrudes from his left fist, like a microphone.

"Any bully hopefuls yet, Bernadette?" asks Charlie into the microphone, still in his announcer's discreet tones.

"No obvious candidates in row one, by the door, or row two," she says, leading Charlie on.

"Isn't this exciting, folks!"

Lewis spares a glance at the back of the class. He'd love to sit there. Cool kids sit at the back. Bored kids. Bad kids. One kid is leaning back so far he's not so much sitting as lying at his desk. His hands are crossed on his chest. Blond hair falls limply in front of his face, like a bridal veil. His boredom is pure enough to be almost an abstract quality.

Bernadette gasps. She can't help it. Frank, the striped-shirted biker they met earlier, has entered the classroom.

"Oh, my," whispers Lewis. He attempts to hide behind Bernadette.

"What is it? Do we have a candidate?" asks Charlie.

"Oh yes."

"Is he big?"

"Head and shoulders bigger than everyone else here. He's having trouble fitting into the desk in the third row. Hard to believe he's in grade seven."

"Does he look mean?"

"I'd say so. The tattoos and piercings help. And the shaved head. And there's the healed scar from a branding iron on the back of one hand. But it's more than that. He's . . . angry. You can almost feel the anger coming out of him like heat."

"Oooh, a brand," says Lewis. "He did that on purpose, didn't he, Bernadette?"

"Either that, or he's been very unlucky near the barbecue."

Lewis shudders again.

"Let's see, what other characteristics mark the typical bully. Is he fat?" asks Charlie. "And *ugly*—whatever that means? Lots of acne?"

"He's chubby, for sure. His backside spills over his chair like . . . I don't know, like Coke spilling over the glass when you pour too fast. But he has quite good skin." Bernadette tries to be objective. "In fact, he could be quite handsome if he lost a bit of weight and if—"

She was going to say, *If only he wasn't so scary,* but at that moment Frank snorts up some phlegm, and then chews it for a moment like gum, moving it around his mouth. His prominent Adam's apple ripples up and down his throat when he finally swallows.

"Of course," she goes on steadily, "there are some personal-hygiene issues as well."

From under his bare and glistening brow, Frank stares at them. A few seconds pass in silence, and then, "Oy," he says. "He's blind!"

He speaks in a clotted mucusy growl, making Bernadette long to clear her throat.

"Blind!" he repeats. "Look at that. The kid can't see! *Haw haw haw haw haw haw haw.*" He has an annoying laugh, strangely high-pitched. He pounds on his desk with his hand. The laugh fades away into a thick cough. He hawks up a good nourishing glassful of mucus and swallows it down again.

There is a collective intake of breath around the room. A brunette in the second row shows a spectacular scowl.

Charlie recaps, back in his TV-announcer persona. "Ladies and gentlemen, this is one serious bully candidate."

Lewis has been watching the whole scene with growing relief. "Yes, he's a bully, but he's not going to terrorize *me.* He's interested in *you,* Charlie. What a great day!" Lewis pummels his fist into his other palm. His glasses shine with joy. Someone else is the victim. "I'm all right!"

"How nice for you," Charlie comments drily.

"Hey, blind kid!" Frank rises to his feet—a lengthy procedure, during which Lewis takes three backward steps. "Are you really blind? Can you see anything?"

Charlie clears his throat. "As a matter of fact, no," he says. "I can't see anything at all."

"Haw haw haw haw." He moves toward Charlie and Bernadette, looming over them like a cliff. He holds his hand in front of Charlie's face. "How many fingers am I holding up?" he asks.

"I don't know."

Bernadette tries to keep herself between the two boys. She stares around the class, looking for possible support. A really cute guy with dimples and sharply creased pants, a fine physical specimen except that he's kind of short, notices her looking at him, blinks nervously, and turns away. She wonders where Mr. Floyd can be.

Lewis leans casually against Adrienne Button-Smith's desk. She's the brunette with the scowl. Also raised eyebrows and braces on her teeth. A superior girl. Lewis grins at her. "Isn't this great!" he says. "Poor Charlie, I'd hate to be him right now."

"I'd hate to be you," says Adrienne.

Meanwhile, at the front of the class, things are coming to a head. Frank reaches out toward Charlie's sunglasses. Bernadette's hand lashes and slaps his hand aside. "That's enough," she says. "Leave him alone."

Silence in the room. The sound of the slap echoes. Bernadette can't take it back. Not that she wants to. She's mad. If the big ape wants a fight, he'll get one. He may kill her, but she's going to go down biting and scratching.

Most of the class is on their feet.

Frank stares at his slapped hand and clenches it into a fist. He glares at Bernadette. She feels in her pocket for a pencil. Watches his eyes. They'll tell her when he's about to move.

The eyes flash. Bernadette pulls out the pencil, prepared to use it.

"Ayyy!" A smooth, twinkly voice from the door. "Ayyy, come on, now. What *is* this?"

All heads turn. A very handsome man leans in the doorway. His smile, wide and white, and his clothes, tight and black, are arresting. His hair, tossed casually back from his high forehead, is arresting. Everything about him is arresting.

"Mr. Floyd?" asks Bernadette.

"Who else, kiddo?" He waggles his eyebrows at her. Bernadette realizes that she has her mouth open. She closes it.

"Come on now, guys," he says again. He glides into the room, swinging a soft leather briefcase. He's almost dancing. "Find yourselves chairs. Okay?"

Bernadette leads Charlie to his seat by the door.

"Hey!" Lewis whispers to Adrienne. "We've got the cool teacher."

"I beg your pardon?"

"You know," Lewis whispers. "The cool teacher. Every school has one. The teacher everyone talks about. The girls think he's cute, and the guys admire him. Didn't your old school have one? Mine did. Mr. Garden. What a great basketball player he was. He was so cool. He called me by name once. 'Hey there, Lewis,' he said. Just like that. I wasn't even in his class. Everyone admired me that day."

Adrienne frowns at him. "You are pathetic," she says.

"Yes, I know." But, inside, Lewis is bursting with pride. He'll be in the cool teacher's class all year.

Charlie always gets the seat nearest the door. He likes to be first out so he doesn't get jostled on the way down the hall. He finds his chair and reaches into his knapsack. The Louis Light 200 is a word-processing and calculating device about the same size and shape as a hardcover book or a box of chocolates but weighing a bit more, say as much as a brick or bowling ball, or a roast loin of pork. It hums under his fingers, warm and alive. "Thanks, Bernie," he whispers. She's sitting behind him. "Was that close, back there?"

"Yeah," she says. "Mr. Floyd saved us. What a cool guy! And he wears nice clothes. I wonder where he gets them. And some kind of men's fragrance."

"That may not be him. I've been smelling my dad's cologne all morning on me. Say, is that Lewis kid nearby?"

"On my left," says Bernadette.

Charlie cocks his head. "I can't hear him."

"He's busy," says Bernadette.

Lewis has squirmed his way near Bernadette and Charlie. Good to be near your friends, right? He has claimed the desk next to Bernadette and leaned over to whisper in her direction, when he feels a hand on his shoulder from behind. A heavy hand. His neighbor on the other side is trying to get his attention. He glances backward into the smiling face of the bully, who smiles ferociously and puts out a hand.

"Name's Frank," he says. "Shake."

Lewis cannot believe it. He's sitting beside the bully again! How did this happen? He knows what will happen if he shakes hands with Frank. "No, thanks," he says. "In fact, now that I think about it, I'll just move. There's a free desk at the front of—"

"Shake!" says Frank. His hand is knobby and gnarled. The brand mark is in the shape of an *X.* Lewis swallows, then slowly, sadly, resignedly holds out his hand. Frank chuckles wetly, grabs Lewis's hand in his, and squeezes.

Lewis cringes, writhes.

"Hey there, you guys!" Mr. Floyd stands at the front of the class with his hands in his pockets. He looks like an ad in a glossy magazine, thinks Bernadette. "Welcome to class 7F and all that crud."

The class giggles. *Crud.* The teacher said *crud.* Wow.

"Sorry I wasn't here to meet you. I'm running a bit late this morning. There was a holdup." His ultrawhite teeth gleam briefly in his face. He picks up an official sheet of paper and a pencil. "I'll begin by taking attendance. They make us do this stuff. Just call out when you hear your name."

"Ow! Ow!" Lewis cannot contain a moan. He cradles his hand against his chest.

Mr. Floyd chuckles without looking up. "Don't call out now. Wait until you hear your name. All right, guys? That's great. Now, Adrienne Button-Smith. Is she here?"

Adrienne sniffs. "Yes," she says.

"That's great!" He still doesn't look up.

Charlie's fingertips touch lightly on the six keys of his Louis Light 200. One key for each of the six spaces in a braille cell. The seventh key is a space bar. Charlie types his name quickly, recapturing the feel of the machine. 614, 125, 1, 1235, 123, 24, 15. The braille cell for the letter *C* is 14—the 6 in front turns it into a capital letter.

The school is on the same time as he is. The bell rings just as the little clock in his head clicks over from 8:59 to 9:00. A loudspeaker crackles, and a grandmotherly voice introduces herself as the principal. Mrs. Vox. Charlie remembers her from the O and M.

"Good morning, boys and girls, and welcome to an exciting new year at Schuyler Colfax Middle School. Please stand now for the national anthem and the Pledge of Allegiance."

Charlie thinks of all the students up and down the country doing exactly—exactly—what he is doing. Standing loosely at attention, mouthing familiar words, thinking ahead to the new school year. At this moment he is just like them.

The announcements are about things like lunch money and sports-team tryouts and letters home. Also rules of behavior. What to wear, how to talk. They call it Appropriate Dress and Demeanor. ADD. Braille cells: 1, 145, 145. Charlie wonders if there's Ritalin for poor dress and demeanor. . . .

"And finally," says Mrs. Vox, "an announcement about a special student. This year, our school contains a student who is . . . visually impaired."

Charlie hears the intake of breath around him. He knows they are staring. He has been stared at all his life. He forces himself to smile. If you don't care, they don't win.

"Visually impaired?" asks a breathy soprano voice from nearby. She hasn't spoken yet.

"It's Charlie, isn't it?" Lewis's voice now. "She's talking about Charlie, isn't she?"

The principal goes on. "I want you all to treat him as you would treat a normal—I mean, any other student. Good luck, Charlie. That's all for now, students. My name is Mrs. Vox, and most of you will be seeing me around the school. You'll be hearing me around, Charlie."

SCENE 7: *Gideon*

"Rachel Danowski," says Mr. Floyd.

"Oh—yes?"

Bernadette wrinkles her nose. She can't help it. Rachel is everything she can't stand in a girl: busty, full-lipped, pretty. A stupid girl, who wears a lot of eye shadow and talks in a breathy soprano. A bimbo. The kind of girl guys like automatically. See—Mr. Floyd is smiling approval at her, even though all she did was recognize her name.

"Charlie Fairmile," calls Mr. Floyd.

"Present," says Charlie.

Rachel stands up to get a better look at Charlie. "Say, is *he* the guy? The . . . impaired guy? He's got a white stick."

"What a bimbo," mutters Bernadette.

"Charlie," says Rachel. "Just like on the announcement. Oh, *righty!* It is him." She smiles seductively at Charlie, licking her lips. She can't help it—it is her natural reaction to guys. When he doesn't react at all, she pouts slightly and sits down. Mr. Floyd watches her. So does Bernadette. Neither of them notices Frank the bully, who is tearing a losing lottery ticket into little paper pellets and flicking them off his thumb at Charlie.

He misses with the first one. And the second.

"Bernadette Lyall," says Mr. Floyd.

She puts up her hand. Will he smile at her the way he did at Rachel? Nope.

Frank fires another pellet and hits Lewis in the back of the head.

All this time the classroom door has been closed. Now it opens from the outside with enough force to slam it against the wall, attracting everyone's attention. The clock clicks over from 9:06 to 9:07.

Framed in the doorway is a stocky boy with crew-cut hair, in a dress vest and baggy shorts.

Mr. Floyd raises his eyebrows. "Who are you?"

"Hey, it's him," Bernadette whispers to Charlie.

"I know. I heard the music again."

"I didn't."

"Are you in this class?" asks Mr. Floyd.

Bernadette frowns. "How come you could hear the music and I couldn't?" she whispers.

"I don't know. Maybe it wasn't for you."

"But I heard it last time. On the street."

"What's your name?" asks Mr. Floyd.

"Gideon," says Gideon.

Mr. Floyd frowns, checks the list in his hand. "Gideon. Oh, sure. Here you are. Hey, man, you're late. Late on the first day. Not too cool."

The class snickers. *Man.* The teacher called Gideon *man.*

"You can take the attendance sheet to the office, okay? Serve you right for coming in late—hey, guys?"

The class laughs obediently.

Gideon turns his head to stare up at the clock. He doesn't say anything.

Mr. Floyd follows Gideon's gaze, and freezes.

The clock on the wall reads 8:59.

"Whoa!" Mr. Floyd shakes his head. "There must be some mistake." He checks his watch, shakes it, holds it up to his ear. "I could have sworn . . . Hey, guys, what time is it?"

The students turn their heads together, check the wall, and answer, "Eight fifty-nine."

Well, not all the students. Charlie consults his internal clock. "Nine-oh-eight," he says.

Mr. Floyd checks his watch again, shakes it next to his ear. He sighs. "Well, someone has to take the attendance form to the office. Gideon, how about you? When you come back you can find yourself a seat."

Lewis has been waiting for an opportunity. "Sir," he says, waving his hand. "Oh, please, Mr. Floyd, sir. Let *me* take the form downstairs, please, sir."

Mr. Floyd frowns. "Who are you again?"

"Lewis, sir. Lewis Ellieff. Eager to help you, sir. And eager for exercise. I always say that a quick walk early in the morning sets you up for the whole day."

Mr. Floyd blinks. "Hey, thanks there, um, Lewis. I—"

Lewis scrambles to his feet. "No, no. Thank *you,* sir. Thank you." He bustles up to the front of the class, takes the form from Mr. Floyd's hand, and heads for the door, stopping on the way to put his arm around Gideon's shoulders. He's taller than Gideon, and adopts a paternal tone.

"Oh, and, uh, Gideon," he says in a low voice, "feel free to take my desk. That one there beside the big bald guy. Nice desk, I'm sure you'll like it. Good location. I'll find another one when I get back." Gideon hesitates, but Lewis pushes him gently. "No, no, I insist. Go on now. Thanks. I mean it."

He heads for the door, whistling. Gideon moves slowly toward Lewis's old desk. The teacher watches him.

The clock clicks over to 9:00. The bell rings, and the principal comes over the public-address system. "Good morning, boys and girls, and welcome to an exciting"—her voice falters—"new year at Schuyler Colfax Middle Public School. Please stand now for the . . . Wait a minute. I'm sure I said this." She clears her throat and goes on doubtfully. "Please stand now for the national anthem and the . . . Pledge of . . . Oh, dear. Oh, dear. That finishes the announcements for this morning, boys and girls. Have a nice day."

Downstairs, in the principal's office, Mrs. Vox, a lovely grandmotherly woman except for her thick dark eyebrows, is lying back in her swivel chair. In her hand is a disposable face wipe. She massages her neck. On the desk is an opened bottle of nonprescription painkillers.

"What's wrong with me today?" she murmurs to herself. "I must be coming down with something."

She looks up to see Muriel, her secretary, standing in the doorway.

"Phone for you, Mrs. Vox," she whispers dramatically. Since she could have simply transferred the call, Mrs. Vox knows there is something exciting about it.

"What wants to talk to me, Muriel?"

"It's the police!" With a sharp intake of breath. Muriel's eyes sparkle.

Mrs. Vox takes another pill from the bottle, then picks up the phone.

Back in the classroom, Mr. Floyd carries the stack of notebooks over to Rachel's desk in the front row. "Pass these out, kiddo," he says.

"Sure, Mr. Floyd." She licks her lips at him.

Gideon takes Lewis's old seat beside Frank. He is the smallest kid in the class. Sitting down, he comes up to the bully's rib cage. His feet barely touch the floor. He relaxes, leans back in his chair, puts his hands behind his head. Frank gloats down at him, the giant contemplating Mickey Mouse. *"Haw haw!"* he says. Gideon winks up at him.

Rachel is handing out notebooks to the first row. She holds one out to Charlie, but he doesn't take it. She frowns. "Hey, Charlie," she says. "Don't you want a notebook?"

"No, thanks," he says. "I've got my keyboard here."

"Huh? Huh?"

Mr. Floyd is writing on the board.

Frank's whisper is wet and nasty. "You're so . . . small!" he says to Gideon. "You're a shrimp! You're nothing! *Haw, haw, haw!*" Frank chokes, swallows. He holds out his hand. "Name's Frank," he says, flexing. "Shake."

"Gideon." They shake. Frank's hand is big enough to engulf Gideon's. The big guy squeezes hard, gritting his back teeth. Sweat forms on his brow and shaved head. Gideon grins. No effort. After a moment Frank takes back his right hand, stares at it, stares at Gideon, and then cradles the hand carefully against his chest.

Mr. Floyd finishes writing on the blackboard. Bernadette reads for Charlie. "The most exciting thing that DIDN'T happen this summer was . . ." she whispers.

"Was what?" asks Charlie.

"Just *was*," she says. "It's going to be an assignment."

Charlie starts typing. The word *the* is an article. He types 134, 135, 234, 235 for the letters of *most* . . .

Rachel turns around to stare. She nods to herself. "Oh?" she says. "Oh, *righty!*"

What a day Lewis is having! All right, the incident with the dog before school was scary, but ever since then it's been, like, the best day ever. Lewis loves where he's sitting. He is no longer beside the big bully. That little kid, Gideon, is sitting there. Weird kid, Gideon. Lewis wonders if he might be worth cultivating. You never know who can help you. Meanwhile, Lewis is at the back of the class.

All of his school life he has wanted to sit here, with the kids who throw spitballs and tell dirty jokes and don't study for tests. Lewis has never sat at the back of the class before. He is enjoying every moment of it.

They're getting their locker assignments. Mr. Floyd is walking up and down the rows, giving out slips of paper with the locker number and lock combination on it. He doesn't just place them on the desk, like a normal teacher. He tosses them casually, like confetti. He is so cool. Imagine having the cool teacher all year! Imagine how it'll be in May, after a year with the cool teacher. . . .

Lewis can see it now: the playground kids nudging one another as he goes by. "Do you know who that is? That's Lewis Ellieff. He's in Mr. Floyd's class. Wow."

He'll smile condescendingly and walk on.

Someone will toss him a Frisbee, which he will catch one-handed and zip back.

There'll be a circle of little kids around the cool teacher. There always is. "Hey, Mr. Floyd!" they'll shout. And Mr. Floyd will wave at them and try to edge away.

When he catches sight of Lewis, he'll give a special smile. "Yo, Lewis," he'll say.

"Yo, Mr. F!" Lewis will call back. The cool teacher at his old school let his class call him G-man. Wouldn't it be great to call Mr. Floyd F-man? Yo, F-man! The playground kids will open their mouths wide and gasp. "F-man! He called Mr. Floyd F-man! Wow."

Lewis leans back in his chair at the back of the classroom, a happy smile playing over his face like summer lightning. He glances casually at the long, skinny, baggy-pants boy who sits beside him. The ultimate bored being. Wayne is his name. He's so bored he is drawing a picture on his own arm.

"Great idea," whispers Lewis. "I'll do that, too. Say, what is that you're drawing?" He leans over to stare. "Monster, hey? Great." The boy doesn't look up from his arm. He's wearing a T-shirt, making the self-tattooing easy. Lewis smiles at him, undoes his cuff link, rolls up his sleeve, and starts in with a pen.

Seems like it's only a few minutes later that the bell rings. Can it be lunch already?

———

They've given Charlie a special lock—it opens with a key rather than a combination. He tries it a couple of times. No problem. Bernadette is beside him. "You can remember which locker is yours?" she asks.

"Sure. It's number two-eighty." The fingers of his left hand go to the number plaque on the front of the locker, touching it lightly. The way he reads things with his fingertips reminds her of a rare jungle animal she saw on the Discovery Channel once. It had the same long delicate fingers, gently probing to decide if a branch was safe or a fruit was edible. Tarsier? Lemur? Something like that. "If that's not enough, I know my locker is exactly fourteen paces left of the classroom door."

Bernadette closes her eyes and tries to read the plaque on her locker with her fingers. They seem fat and awkward. Can she feel the number 281? She concentrates hard, putting all her mind into her fingertips.

"What is it, are you blind, too, now?"

Frank's mouth is open wide. His eyes glitter. He laughs meanly. "Blindness must be catching," he says. "Like cooties. *Haw haw haw.*"

"Ha-ha," she says.

He tries the lock beside Charlie's.

Oh dear NO, she thinks. This cannot be happening, she thinks. Charlie won't make it through a whole year with his locker next to Frank's. Neither will I.

Frank spins the lock. His smell is strong and sour. "You hit me," he says. He's not laughing now. "Back there . . . in the classroom . . . you hit me."

She doesn't say anything. He's so big.

"No girl hits me," he says then, leaning past her. "No blind guy either."

"Is he talking about me?" says Charlie, his hand on Bernadette's arm.

"Shhh," she says.

The lock on Frank's locker won't open. He tries it again, muttering the numbers. Nothing. He swears. Tries it one more time. Nope. He hits the locker with his hand, hard enough to make another dent in the metal. "Who does this locker belong to anyway?" he says.

"Gideon," says Gideon.

Where'd he come from? But there he is, crew cut, vest, baggy shorts, grin. He's tossing one of his little bouncy balls from hand to hand. He puts the ball in his pocket and, with absolutely no effort at all, pushes Frank out of the way.

Bernadette stares. It's like watching a midget move a mountain, but the mountain moves all the same.

"Hey!" cries Frank. "Hey! You! What are you doing?"

He grabs Gideon and shoves hard. Nothing happens. Gideon twists the combination lock to the right, stops, and spins it left.

Frank bends down to pick Gideon up. He's got to be twice

the size of the little guy. Gideon is smiling the whole time. He spins the lock to the right, pulls open the hasp. He smiles up at Frank.

Frank can't budge Gideon. He's got his arms under the little guy's shoulder blades and is straining mightily, but nothing is happening. Is the little guy too heavy to lift? Gideon checks the inside of the locker, places one of his bouncy balls inside it, shuts the door, and locks it.

"Say, um, Gideon—is that your locker?" asks Bernadette.

Gideon nods.

"So where's mine?" Frank scowls hugely. "Where is my locker?" He kicks the one nearest him and moves away.

Bernadette and Charlie discuss what to do about Frank on the way downstairs. They don't have any answers. "We'll have to get a plan," says Bernadette. "After all, the little guy won't always be there to help us."

"What little guy?"

"Gideon?" says Gideon. He has snuck up on them and follows them down the stairs.

"Jeez, don't do that!" says Bernadette.

He grins up at them, a cocky kid with crew-cut hair and a wad of gum in his mouth. Something about his eyes has been bothering her all day. She sees it now. They don't go with the rest of him. They are older than he is. It's like an old man is staring out of a kid's face.

"Say," asks Charlie, pausing on the stairs, turning his head toward the other boy, "this is not a knock, but I've been meaning to ask. Can you say anything apart from—"

"Gideon?" says Gideon.

"Yeah."

"Sure," says Gideon.

Bernadette stares at him. Who is he? What is he? She really cannot figure him out.

He holds the door for Bernadette and Charlie. Charlie wrinkles his nose, going past. "Do you smell cologne, Gideon?" he asks.

"Sure," says Gideon.

"Yo, Charlie, Bernadette, how you doing?" asks Lewis. He and a tall kid from class stroll up to them on the playground. Lewis has his hands in his pockets.

"*Yo?*" Bernadette is puzzled. What's with him? "*Yo* yourself."

"We're just fine," says Charlie.

"Lunch recess, my favorite time of day," says Lewis. He sounds elaborately casual. "No work to be done at recess. Not that I do a lot of work during class, heh heh. As you can see." He holds out his arm.

"What *is* that?" she asks. "What have you done to yourself?"

"Just a little scribbling. Some of us don't pay a lot of attention, hey, Wayne? You guys know Wayne." Lewis jerks his shoulder at his companion.

"Hi, Wayne," says Charlie. Bernadette nods. Wayne yawns across the playground over the tops of their heads.

"Wayne and I sit at the back of the class," says Lewis. "Regular troublemakers we are." He elbows Wayne in the ribs. "Tough guys, that's us!" Wayne wanders away without saying good-bye. Lewis watches him, shaking his head. "There's a free spirit," he says.

Bernadette is still staring at Lewis's forearm. "You won't believe this, Charlie," she says. "He's drawn all over his arm, in pen. Pictures of . . . I don't know. Circles and stars and stuff."

"Why?" asks Charlie.

"Ritual signs," says Lewis. "Like tribal scars. Wayne has them, too. When you sit at the back of the class, you got to belong. You have to look tough."

"But," says Charlie, "you aren't tough. Are you?"

"Tough enough," says Lewis, with a slight cock of his head.

"What's this here?" Bernadette pulls his wrist toward her for a better look. "Is that a happy face?" She laughs. "It is! It's a *happy face!*"

Lewis blushes, hides his arm behind his back. "I got distracted," he says.

"A happy face! Tough marking, O great warrior. What's your secret tribal name? *Runs To Mama? Eats From Kids' Menu? Plays With LEGOs?*"

"Hey—don't knock LEGOs," says Charlie.

"Wayne has a skull and crossbones," says Lewis. "Like a pirate or something."

Wayne is over on the basketball court with the other tall kids. Bernadette watches him fold himself up like a lawn chair to sit down. Pirate, all right.

They wander over to the fence to look out at traffic. The accident from earlier this morning has been cleared away, but a police car is still on the scene.

"Cops," says Lewis, out of the side of his mouth. "Bastards!" He spits.

Charlie smiles. "When you get into a role, you really get into it, don't you."

"Careful," says Bernadette.

"Shoot. Hang on." Lewis has dribbled spit on himself. He leans forward, wiping his face furtively with a hand. "Anyone got a Kleenex?"

SCENE 9: *Monsieur Noël*

Mr. Floyd draws a story diagram on the board. It looks like half of a mountain, or a graph showing that a company has had a successful third quarter. He explains that their writing assignment should follow this pattern. As the story moves along, it should get more and more exciting, he says.

"I don't understand," Rachel's pearly white top teeth rest on her bee-stung lower lip. "You told us to write about something exciting that didn't happen this summer. I don't get that. I mean, I went to camp for a week. I visited my auntie in Cleveland. Apart from that, I, uh, watched TV and went to the movies with my friends. I hung around and worked on my tan. Is that exciting?"

Snickering from the back of the class. Wayne asks if he can see Rachel's tan line.

The whole class laughs out loud. Lewis pounds Wayne on the back. "Funny guy," he says. "Funny guy back here."

"So, what should I do?" asks Rachel. "The truth is boring."

Mr. Floyd's eyes blaze suddenly. "Change it, then," he says. "That's the point of the assignment. Change your life. Learn to lie!"

Gasps from some of the class. Charlie remembers his dad saying that Mr. Floyd's teaching style was innovative.

"But lying is bad, isn't it?" asks Rachel.

"Lies are powerful!" says Mr. Floyd. "Think of the jokes that make you laugh—they're lies. Chickens don't really cross the road. Elephants don't really hide in trees. Do they, Rachel?"

"Well, no."

"Think of the ghost stories that keep you up at night, or the nasty things people say to make you mad. All lies." He looks around the class, taking them all in. He cares about this, thinks Bernadette. More to the point, it's interesting.

"Think on a larger scale. Lie about it. Think of so-called universal truths. *All men are created equal*—a lie. *The best things in life are free*—a lie. *The one true faith*—a lie, no matter who says it. These lies are powerful enough to have started wars. *Jumbo shrimp*—a lie. How can there be jumbo shrimp? Think about it."

He's smiling now, taking the edge off his argument. The class is happy to smile back.

"Isn't there something you've always wanted to do, Rachel? Something you wished you had done?"

She swallows. "Well, sure, I guess. There was that time at camp I—"

He holds up his hand. "That's the assignment. Write about that!"

"Okay." She still sounds doubtful.

"They're putting you in a box, Rachel. Don't let them do it to you. I hate people putting me in a box. Middle-aged box. Teacher box. I hate people knowing what I do, where I go. Home. School. Gym. Supermarket."

"You go to the gym?" says Rachel.

He stands at the front of the class, arms outstretched. "Take your summer, Rachel, and *make* it exciting. Lie about it. Think of something you could have done. Something you wanted to do. Like . . . discovering treasure. Do you understand?"

Of course she doesn't, thinks Bernadette. She's a bimbo. Gazing up at him, batting her lashes.

"Do you really go to the gym, Mr. Floyd? 'Cause you look like you do. You're real, you know, fit-looking."

Kissing noise from the back row. The class snickers loudly.

"Funny guy back here!" says Lewis.

Last period of the day is French. Bernadette's heart stops when the teacher walks into the classroom and smiles at her. The feeling lasts only a moment. *"Bonjour, mes élèves,"* he says, and she realizes that he is not her dad.

But does he ever look like him! Incredibly like him: a rumpled, middle-aged, fattish guy with dark hair slicked back and eyes that crinkle at the corners. Same way of holding his head on one side. Same sharp nose in the middle of the round face, like a knife blade in the middle of a cheese ball. She wishes she'd inherited that kind of nose, instead of her mother's rounded nub. Almost the same smile, though she can see now that the teeth are whiter and closer together than her father's.

It must have been this guy in the staff parking lot this morning. No wonder she thought she was seeing things. The resemblance is very striking.

His name is Monsieur Noël. *"Comme le père Noël,"* he says with a nervous smile. "You know, Santa Claus." He has an accent like a hockey player from Quebec.

Bernadette sighs, remembering a Christmas morning two or maybe three years ago. Dad knocked on the apartment door early, unshaven and smelling of breath mints. He had a neatly wrapped present for her, and he flopped down in the big chair to watch her open it. She doesn't remember what the present was. Barbie doll? No. Even he knew she was too old for dolls. But something almost as inappropriate: a make-your-own-jewelry kit, or girlie pink pajamas in the wrong size. And she unwrapped as slowly and carefully as she could, one corner at a time, trying to lift the folds without ripping the professionally applied wrapping paper, because she knew he'd go away as soon as she'd opened her gift.

"Bonjour, mes élèves!"

"Bonjour, Monsieur Noël."

"Bien dit. Eh, maintenant, nous pouvons—" The teacher stops. His eyes are on the door. *"Bonjour, mesdames."*

"Mrs. Vox and some other woman have just come in," Bernadette whispers to Charlie.

"What's the other woman like?"

"Don't know. They're talking to Monsieur Noël. She's got a brown suit. Looks tough but nice. Something's wrong. He's upset."

Monsieur Noël's hand is at his mouth in a classic gesture of distress.

"Why?" whispers Charlie.

It is the woman in brown who is causing the French teacher to panic. She is a police detective named Perry. Monsieur Noël has seventy-odd unpaid parking tickets, with fines totaling almost nine thousand dollars (a hefty ticket nestles in his jacket pocket right now—he picked it up this morning for parking in a handicapped spot), and he is afraid of being tracked down and prosecuted.

Mrs. Vox introduces Detective Perry to the students and stands back to let her speak.

"Excuse the interruption, boys and girls." Perry has a snappy voice, precise and resonant, like she's speaking from inside a snare drum. "I'm heading up Captain Davicki's team, and I don't have a lot of time. I was hoping your teacher could help me. . . ."

"Teacher?" Monsieur Noël whimpers. *"C'est moi."* His fears have materialized. The police have caught up with him. "Is it . . . an arrest?" he says.

"Arrest?" snaps Perry. "What do you know about an arrest, sir?"

Monsieur Noël staggers back against his desk. "I'm very sorry," he says. His accent thickens, so that *very* sounds like *vairee.* "I didn't know it was a 'andicapped spot."

Perry stares at him. "I beg your pardon?"

"I didn't see the . . . the sign! And I was only parked for a few minutes. Now I am a criminal. A criminal! *Moi.* My papa was right. *Je suis imbécile!"*

Monsieur Noël is sitting dejectedly at his desk, his head in his hands.

"What are you talking about?"

"Aren't you here because of my parking tickets?" he moans.

"Parking? I don't care about parking."

"You don't?" He lifts his head, his face pinkening and lightening like the dawn sky.

"Of course not. I'm with Major Crimes."

"And tickets—parking tickets—a few unpaid parking tickets—are not major crimes? Of course not. *Heu heu heu!*"

"Park wherever you can. Parking's a mess in this city. I use fire hydrants myself. No. I'm here to pick up a student. Fairmile."

Monsieur Noël wipes his forehead with a large white handkerchief.

Mrs. Vox clears her throat. "Charlie Fairmile."

Charlie sits very still. It's his way, Bernadette knows. He reacts by not reacting. She puts up her hand.

Mrs. Vox touches the detective's arm, whispers in her ear.

Bernadette remembers where she has heard the name Davicki before. He's in charge of the Stocking Bandit investigation. What can the police want with Charlie? she wonders.

"Charles Fairmile, could you come with us?" says Detective Perry.

"Bernadette, you come, too," says Mrs. Vox.

"Both of you come," says the detective.

Bernadette gathers her stuff, makes sure Charlie doesn't leave his Louis Light 200 behind.

"What about my educational assistant?" he asks. "Mr. Underglow is going to help me with my homework."

"Believe me," says the detective with some sympathy, "homework is not your biggest problem right now."

Charlie hangs on to Bernadette's elbow. They're in the hall. Classroom noises all around them, fading as they pass. Conversations, mostly. He hears, clear as crystal, someone burping, and a teacher asking who made that noise. He hears the detective saying something to Mrs. Vox.

Smell of unwashed hair. And fruit candy. And, faintly, cigarette smoke. Very pungent, tobacco. Not on the policewoman's breath. Maybe on her clothes.

Momentary smell of disinfectant, and sweat, and dirty water. Janitor pushing a bucket on wheels. One of them squeaks.

Smell of tuna fish. Someone's lunch leftovers in a locker.

Downstairs and through the front hall—the echo of their footsteps sounds totally different here—to the outside world. Smell of warm pavement and car exhaust. Sun on his right cheek.

"Hurry," snaps the detective. "Get in."

Get in what? Car, probably. Bernadette takes Charlie's hand and places it on the plush seat. Yep, car. She pushes his head lower, helps him in. He slides ahead of her.

"Is this a real police car?" he whispers.

"No. It's a plain dark Ford. Two-way radio in the front, though."

"Good luck, Charlie," says Mrs. Vox. "I'm so sorry for you. I'm sure it will all work out."

"Me, too," says Charlie.

The car drives away.

"Where are you taking us?" asks Charlie over the noise of the car engine and the traffic and the crackling radio.

"Police station," is the answer. "Fifty-second Precinct."

"Why?"

"To see your mom. We may have a couple of questions for you, too," she replies. Her radio crackles. Something about arrival. "Perry," she says loudly. Probably into the radio. "Tell the captain we'll be arriving in ten minutes. Over and out."

"Why would you want to question us?" asks Bernadette.

"Why is Mom at the police station?" asks Charlie.

"She's with the—that is, your father," says the detective.

Bernadette grips his hand. Charlie blinks. Nothing. He feels nothing. Certainly not fear. It's too bizarre.

The car lurches around a corner. Charlie is thrown against the door. He must be more upset than he realizes. Usually he braces himself better than this.

"Sorry, kid," says the detective.

———

The police station smells of smoke and dirt and fear. Kind of like school, come to think of it, only more so, as if the emotions of school are purified and concentrated here.

"Charlie! Oh, Charlie!"

His mother's voice. He hurries toward it, forcing Bernadette to run to keep up.

"What's wrong, Mom?"

Her hands are trembly in his.

"It's your father, Charlie. He's been here all morning. The police think . . . I can hardly say it!" She sobs.

"What?"

"They think he may be the Stocking Bandit."

SCENE 9A: *Captain Davicki*

When the police *think* you're the bad guy, but don't know for sure, they bring you to the station and ask you a lot of questions. That's what's happening to Roger Fairmile now. He's sitting in an interview room going over his story again.

"So where is the money now?" asks another detective—the fourth or fifth he's seen.

"I don't know what you're talking about."

"Money, Roger. From the other cash-machine robberies. A total of almost a quarter of a million dollars, the banks say."

"I didn't rob any other cash machines."

The detective checks his list of questions.

"So, how'd you get to the bank this morning, Roger?"

"I took a cab."

"Rich, are you? Take a lot of cabs?"

"I said it before. I was running late. I took a cab because I was late for work."

"You don't look rich."

The police case against Roger is based on a couple of coincidences. Eyewitnesses to the robbery—there were three of these, waiting in line to use the bank machine—described a tall man getting out of a taxi and rushing into the bank to attack the machine. When asked if there was anything else, any other way of distinguishing the tall man, one of the witnesses mentioned a dark suit.

"And an ax," said the second witness.

The police officer taking statements asked if there was anything else. At which point the third witness opened her mouth and pointed out the glass front door of the bank.

"He looked like *that*," said the witness, openmouthed. "Exactly like that."

The policeman turned to see Roger getting out of a taxi. A tall man in a dark suit.

"Say, that *is* him!" the first witness agreed. "Or just like him! Except that he had a sock mask on."

"And an ax," said the second witness.

The taxi drove away, but the police detained Roger. When they found the black sock in his trouser pocket, they took him away.

In an office down the hall from Roger's interview room, Captain Davicki is growling at Detective Perry. Davicki has a good raspy growl. It suits him, goes with his rumpled jackets, uncut hair, scuffed shoes. He looks like a local politician, or a history professor at a small college, or your uncle Walter. Many criminals have underestimated him.

"The commissioner wants an arrest, Perry," he growls. "It's been two months, and we've got nothing. If I say we've captured the Stocking Bandit, she'll stop yelling at me."

"But Fairmile may not be the Stocking Bandit, sir."

Davicki sits on the corner of his desk, hands clasped in front of him. "There's a press conference in twenty minutes. I could announce that we have captured the bandit."

"Please don't, sir. We don't have a weapon. We can't find the money. We can't even find the cab. The idiot driver took off as soon as Fairmile stepped out. It's too soon, sir. We haven't been able to break his story in interrogation. Let us investigate him for a bit."

The phone rings. Davicki raises a bushy eyebrow. "That'll be the commissioner. What'll I tell her?"

"Tell the truth, sir. We have a suspect who is helping us with our inquiries."

"Tell the truth? The *truth?*" He snorts, amused. "What kind of cop are you, Perry?" He picks up phone.

SCENE 9B: *Junior*

The man the police are looking for—the real Stocking Bandit—lets himself into the apartment he shares with his father. A smell of mildew and spices. The curtains are drawn. The September sunshine does not penetrate any part of the living space. "Hello!" he calls. "It's me, Daddy. How did your day go?"

The old man doesn't reply. He spends the whole day watching TV. He never phones anyone, never goes out. The bandit keeps pestering him to get some fresh air, but he never does anything about it. Who'd get old, if they could help it?

"Did you see me on the news, Daddy?" he asks. "I'm famous again. Another daring robbery!" He hangs up a fashionable case, a little too small for a garment bag. Inside is a plain dark banker's suit, and a stocking mask.

He walks to the living-room doorway. The old man is still there. His whole weight is on the table. He hasn't moved since breakfast. The television flickers quietly. The bandit pats his father a couple of times, just to let him know he's there. "Yes, it was all terribly exciting. A woman waiting at the bank machine stared at me with big dark eyes. I'll never forget them. 'You're . . . him!' she said. Then I lifted the ax, and she screamed—" He stops. He doesn't want to tell Daddy about the ax yet.

The old man doesn't turn, doesn't acknowledge his son's presence. The bandit swallows a couple of times. So tough being in the same room as Daddy.

He walks to the kitchen and gets a bottle of malt whiskey, two glasses, and some ice cubes. He pours ice cubes into the glasses, swirls them around, and dumps them into the sink. Then, carefully, he pours whiskey for his father and himself. He carries the drinks into the living room and solemnly raises his glass.

"Come on, Daddy. Drink up. You always liked cash money. And now you'll have lots. You might be grateful, or excited. Aren't you excited?"

Still no response. It's been so long since the old man got excited about anything.

The bandit tries again. "Yes, it's all coming together for you. A fortune, a famous son, and a new place to live! Are you looking forward to the move? Are you? You'll find the money then." He laughs, a bit bitterly. Is that an answering laugh from the old man? Hard to tell. The bandit takes a gulp of his drink.

"There is one piece of bad news, Daddy. I lost your ax. I'm sorry. It wasn't my fault. I had it in the cab, and then I turned around and it was gone!"

Silence.

"Come on, Daddy. It doesn't matter to you. You'll be moving on Friday anyway. Please don't be upset."

His father won't touch his drink. Punishing him. Oh dear.

"Your new place, Daddy. Come on! Let's drink to it."

He raises his glass. His father doesn't.

"You can't beat the location, and you'll be with a whole lot of people just like you. Believe me, you'll fit right in."

He bends over to clink glasses with his dad, who seems unimpressed by the whole ritual. In fact, the bandit has not seen him move since he got home.

Suddenly it's too much. The TV remote is sitting on the table. He grabs it and turns off the set. No reaction. Not a flicker, not a sound. The bandit tries to reason with himself. Take it easy, he thinks. He's old and deaf. He's got nothing. So give him a break. But he can't stand it anymore. He grabs his father's glass and drains it. The liquor burns like a river of fire down to his stomach, warming him, steeling him to tell his father the truth.

"Dammit, Daddy. You're too cheap to live. I can hardly wait to get rid of you. Yes, that's what's really going on. I'm shipping you off. Now, do you want to come to the kitchen and watch me make dinner? Do you? You don't? You *don't?*

Well, that's tough. You're coming anyway, you crazy old coot. I love you, and you're going to watch me make dinner! We're having Madras chicken—spicy, the way you like it. Yum-yum. Now come on!"

He picks him up in one hand and carries him to the kitchen table. Urn and ashes together don't weigh very much. He switches on the stove, drops some grease into a pan, and starts peeling onions.

SCENE 10: *Dinner*

Charlie and his mom at dinner, just the two of them. Dad is still downtown, cooperating with the police. Mom has warmed up leftover stew from yesterday and added, maybe, dumplings. They're a little gooey, but the stickiness makes them easy to pick up on his fork. Charlie hopes they are dumplings. Mom is so upset, who knows what she might have cooked?

It's been a slow evening. No homework on the first day of school, and anyway he couldn't do it until his EA converts his braille files. Mom talks in repetitive rambling sentences, then stops and doesn't say anything for a long time. Charlie focuses on the bite in his mouth right now. Beef, carrot, peppery sauce . . . dumpling?

"He was running late, this morning," she says dully, "so he took a cab, which is expensive, but he didn't want to be late for work, and now they think Roger is the Stocking Bandit. They sounded so sure. How can they be sure?"

She sounds like the mechanical PAWS voice on Charlie's computer.

Other scents around the dinner table include cleaner of some kind, dust, and something moist and nasty from inside the drains. Also his mother's face powder and his father's cologne, left over from breakfast.

Charlie finishes his plate and gets to his feet. His mother is still talking. "If only he hadn't had the sock in his pocket. And if he hadn't gotten butter on his shirtsleeve. If only . . ."

"Can I get some more stew, Mom? It's really good." Charlie walks the three paces to the counter and reaches carefully. He can hear his mother breathing. Where's the serving spoon? He concentrates and reaches confidently. Ha! There it is! His hand closes around the spoon, right there on the counter beside the stove. He knew where it was. Now for the stew pot. He can smell it nearby, hear it bubbling quietly. He concentrates hard and reaches with his free hand.

Lewis's family eat dinner together, in the dining nook at the short end of the L-shaped living room. Mr. and Mrs. Ellieff sit at the north and south ends of the table, with Lewis seated between them. Always between them.

"I made two new friends at school today," he tells them. "Charlie and Bernadette. He's blind. Has a white cane and everything. They live on Copernicus Street, in the same building. We're kind of like the Three . . . Three Musketeers."

He breaks off. His mother puts a steaming platter in the middle of the table. He recognizes the smell. So does his father, who glares across the table at his wife.

"Why'd you cook cabbage rolls?" he asks. Mr. Ellieff is a short balding man, sweating in his undershirt. "Huh? Why'd you go and do that?"

He picks up the platter and slides a couple of cabbage rolls onto his plate.

Mrs. Ellieff pats her helmet of honey golden hair into place and settles her dress around her tightly corseted hips. "You like cabbage."

"Cabbage gives me gas." He finds the largest cabbage roll and adds it to his plateful. "You know that. We've been married fifteen years, you know that cabbage gives me gas."

"If you ate less, you wouldn't get gas. Lewis, take some cabbage rolls before your father finishes them. Take some bread. Take some butter. You've got to keep up your strength."

Mr. Ellieff chews heavily. "If I ate less? Ate less? Are you calling me a pig?"

Lewis spreads butter on a thick slice of bread.

"I'm not calling you a pig. I'm saying that if you ate less, you wouldn't get gas."

"You want to hear me belching all over the place, okay. But it's no fun for me." He glares down at his plate. "No fun at all!"

Lewis takes two cabbage rolls, hands the serving dish to his mother. She adds another cabbage roll to his plate. "You're a growing boy," she says, patting his cheek.

"Aw, Ma, I don't need—"

"Listen to you, woman! His plate is fuller than mine, but he's a growing boy and I'm a pig. You're a hypocrite, that's what you are! A hypocrite!" He belches loudly.

"Listen to me?" Mrs. Ellieff is not in the least cowed by her husband. "Listen to *me*? Listen to you!"

"It's your fault!" he shouts. "You know what cabbage does to me!"

"You don't have to eat so much!"

"I just started, and I'm already a balloon!" He belches again.

"Pig!"

"Hypocrite!"

The Ellieff apartment is full of knickknacks. Lewis eats doggedly, staring at a porcelain dalmatian. He tallies up the spots, chewing in time to his count. He wonders where he can go tonight, to get away.

His mother takes her first bite of cabbage roll. His father has somehow managed to finish all three of his. He reaches for the bread. Silence crackles around the table like lightning in a summer sky. Lewis can't understand why his parents fight so much. Sometimes it seems as if they actually like it.

His mother wipes her mouth with her napkin and puts her hand on his arm. "What did you say about your new friends, dear?" she asks in a very aspartame voice, artificially sweet. She's talking to him, but she's staring daggers down the table at his dad.

"Bernadette and Charlie? I don't know. They like me, I think."

"Of course they do," she says. "You're a very likable boy. You remind me of me when I was your age. All the boys liked me."

"Ha!" cries her husband.

"They did." She smiles at a memory.

"You? Likable? That's a joke! You—" He means to say "hypocrite," but burps in the middle of the word.

"Hippo? What are you saying? Hippo? *You're* the hippo!" she fires back at him.

Can blind people answer the phone? Lewis wonders. He could go to Charlie's place tonight. It'd be better than this.

His parents keep yelling. His dad's face is covered in sweat. He points with the butter knife. "Fifteen years!" he says. "How did I last this long? If it weren't for my boy here, I'd—"

"*Your* boy? He's not yours. He's mine!"

"What do you mean by that?"

"Oh!" Her mouth opens wide. Her eyes flash fire. "Oh, you're impossible!"

Unfortunately, he can't remember Charlie's last name. But Bernadette's falls into his head at once. He can hear Mr. Floyd calling it out: Bernadette Lyall.

Lewis wonders if she's in the phone book.

Bernadette and her mother are eating their dinner in front of the local news when the phone rings. Microwave chicken with rice and a strange orange sauce, 240 calories, eaten straight from the container to save dishes. Cherie is hunched over the coffee table, eating with gusto.

"Ha-ha!" She points at the TV with her fork. "There he is again."

Another newscast. She's been flipping from channel to channel. All the local stations are running the same images of the man suspected to be the Stocking Bandit. There's one grainy three-second clip taken from the security camera as the robbery was in progress, several confusing shots of uniforms converging on a dark-suited man in the main doorway to the bank, and some clearer footage in front of the police station.

"Please, Mom. That's Charlie's dad."

"I know. I know."

The TV is the biggest thing in the living area of the Lyall apartment. The couch is next biggest. Bernadette sits as far from her mom as she can on the couch.

"I know. I know. He looks awful!" Cherie raises the volume. "Doesn't he look awful, Bernadette?" She sounds gleeful. The prospect of someone else in trouble—someone she knows—is so soothing.

The reporter calls him an unidentified man.

"An unidentified man, Steve? Not to me. I know him," cries Cherie, chewing noisily. Steve Metworthy is the newsman, a big-jawed guy with flat, thick blond hair. He looks like he's got a Rice Krispies square on his head.

In her mind, Bernadette is back on the bus this morning. So that really was the Stocking Bandit coming out of the bank. Not a movie. Not a dream. Weird. Now for the big question: Was it Charlie's dad? She tries to focus on the running figure. Dark suit and mask. That was all—two or three seconds at most. The whole sequence was so fast and blurred, so surreal, she doubted her own eyes. No wonder eyewitnesses sound confused all the time.

Charlie's dad? *Mr. Fairmile?* Couldn't have been. Could it?

"Two hundred and forty thousand dollars! Did you hear that? And Gladys doesn't even get earrings out of it. Men are such pigs. Sure, they act like a happy couple, but he's probably got someone on the side. Some little thing with a new diamond choker."

"Mom, please." Bernadette is picking at her food. "What if Mr. Fairmile is innocent?" This is her nightmare—accused of something she didn't do and unable to prove it.

"Hey, what if he's guilty? Weren't you paying attention? There were witnesses. Witnesses identified him at the crime scene. He was still wearing the dark suit. He had a stocking in his pocket. A stocking! Come on, missy."

The screen shows Mr. Fairmile pushed into a waiting police car. A lawyer is standing next to him. She gets in the way, so the camera focuses on her. She has red lips and big eyes. The TV switches to a press conference, a rumpled man in front of a microphone. CAPTAIN DAVICKI is the caption.

"Imagine living down the hall from the Stocking Bandit." Cherie still can't believe it. "I'll have to tell Edna down at the Money Mart. Say, aren't you going to finish your dinner?"

The rice is gooey, and the sauce is congealing in one corner of the cardboard container. Bernadette takes a small, chewy orange forkful, stirs the sauce around, frowns. The TV channel goes to a commercial about travel. There's a picture of the Eiffel Tower.

"That reminds me, Mom. It's really strange, but today at school I saw our French teacher . . . and, well, he looks a lot like Dad."

"What?" Cherie turns with her knife and fork raised in the air, like weapons. Bernadette retreats down the couch.

"It's okay, Mom."

"What did you say? Did you see . . . him . . . at school today? Is he hanging around? Are you seeing him secretly?"

Now Bernadette is confused. "What are you talking about? Dad?"

"Don't mention his name around here."

The TV news has cut to another commercial, a pretty young woman singing around the house because her clothes are so clean.

SCENE 11: *Carol*

Charlie hears the knock over the sad violins. Bernadette always knocks the same way: two fast and then two slow. Charlie opens the door for her and is surprised. There's someone with her. In addition to the usual Bernadette smells—toothpaste, shampoo, her mom's cigarettes—there's a hint of cabbage. Sound of quick breathing and then a familiar voice.

"Hi there, Charlie. So this is where you live. What is it, two-bedroom place? Not bad. Not bad at all. Say, Bernadette told me about your dad. That's amazing! My mom watches Steve Metworthy's evening news. I can't wait to tell her I know the name of the unidentified man."

"Hi there, Lewis," says Charlie. "Cabbage for dinner?"

"Huh? Yes. Cabbage rolls. Why? How did you know?"

Charlie shrugs. "Hi, Bernie."

"Hi, Charlie. How are you? Hey, are you hurt?"

"You mean this?" He holds up his bandaged left hand. "It's nothing. I burned myself on a stew pot. So, what's going on? Do you guys want to come in or go out?"

"We could go out, I guess," says Bernadette.

"Want to go to The Pantry?" Charlie would be happy to get out of here for a bit. It's horrible to think of Dad as a police suspect. And Mom isn't helping.

"How are you really?" asks Bernadette.

"I don't know."

Poor Charlie sounds lost, she thinks. He's usually so calm, so controlled.

"Stew pot, eh?" says Lewis. "I remember once I burned my hand on an element. My ma called Pa out of work, and he had to take me to the hospital. Whoo-ee, I heard about that!"

Charlie walks to the kitchen doorway to tell his mom he's going out. "We'll be down the street at The Pantry," he says into the room. "It's seven-twelve now—I should be home by nine."

"Helping them with their inquiries." Mom's voice comes from the direction of the table. She hasn't moved since dinner. "Helping the police. That's good, isn't it—helping? I asked the lawyer. She was sure it was good."

Charlie goes back to the hall. Bernadette puts his stick and coat in his hands. He thanks her and turns toward the faint smell of cabbage.

"Come on, Lewis."

Charlie hangs on to Bernadette's arm all the way down in the elevator. She checks her jeans pocket for the five-dollar bill that was there yesterday. She hasn't used it. She figures Lewis won't have any money.

In the lobby they run into Mrs. Yodelschmidt. "Have you seen this dog?" she asks them. "Sorry, Charlie, not you, of course, but you other kids? This is my dog."

"Is Casey missing, Mrs. Yodelschmidt?" asks Charlie. "I'm sorry to hear that."

"He's a good dog," says Bernadette. "I'm sure he'll come back."

"We've been together a long time," says Mrs. Yodelschmidt. She's still wearing her fur coat. Also sparkly rings on two or three fingers.

A gusty night. Windy, but it doesn't feel like rain. Charlie taps down the apartment walkway confidently. Bernadette and Lewis are talking behind him. A car drives by with the radio blaring. Sounds of the city rise and swirl around Charlie like warm bathwater. Comforting, satisfying, familiar. There's a squeal of brakes down the street. A car door slams. Voices are raised in anger. Charlie smiles. The pavement changes. Sidewalk now. Turn right, head downhill toward Grant Street.

"Hey, wait up!" calls Bernadette. She and Lewis hurry up

to him. "Sorry, Charlie," she says, putting his left hand on her right elbow.

"No problem. This is the way to The Pantry, right? Who has money?"

"I have lots," says Lewis. "My pa gave me five dollars to make my ma feel bad. Then she gave me ten to make him feel worse. This treat is on me."

The Pantry is a couple of blocks below the cemetery, between a video store and a tattoo parlor. It has a selection of newspapers and desserts and coffees. Charlie and Bernadette like it because it's nearby, and because the waitresses let you sit for hours even if all you've ordered is a Coke and a doughnut. They know all the waitresses. This evening it's Carol, a skinny brunette with three nose rings linked together so that they jingle like a Christmas tree ornament when she shakes her head. She shakes her head to avoid saying no, which she doesn't want to do. Carol's very nice.

The three of them take the corner booth, with a view of the street. Charlie and Bernadette on one side, Lewis on the other. She orders apple crêpes and tea. Charlie orders chocolate milk and a butter tart. He wrinkles his nose up, turning his head left and right. Then he begins folding the napkin in front of him, the way he usually does.

Lewis points down at the menu. "What's this here?"

Carol smiles over her shoulder. "Oh, that's one of our most popular desserts. It's a chocolate mousse cake, with chocolate icing and a chocolate truffle on top. It's served with a chocolate sauce and chocolate shavings."

"Uh-huh," says Lewis. "Pretty chocolaty."

"Yes, sir. That's why it's called Smothered in Chocolate."

"Smothered?"

"Yes, sir. See?" She reaches to push his hand out of the way.

"Oh, I see. My thumb was covering the *S*. I thought it was called 'Mothered in Chocolate.' Mothered, not Smothered. Not that there's much difference." He shudders. "Anyway, I still don't know what to order . . . Say. What's that? What's he eating?" Lewis points across the room.

Bernadette follows his finger and gets a surprise. "It's Uriah!" she says. "Hi, Uriah!"

The vagrant, whose usual spot is the sidewalk in front of their apartment house, waves from behind a table covered with different types of dessert.

"That's the smell," says Charlie. He finishes folding the napkin into a fleur-de-lis and pushes it away from him. "I recognized it when we came in, but didn't believe it. So begging in the street is working for him? Good."

"He flashed a big bill," says Carol, "and ordered half the menu."

"But what is he eating right now?" asks Lewis.

"Mass Appeal Butter Pie," says Carol. She points it out for him on his menu.

"Good thing you didn't have your thumb on that one," murmurs Charlie.

"I'll try the pie," says Lewis, "and a chocolate milk."

Carol makes a point of taking Charlie's hand and putting it on his chocolate milk so he doesn't knock it over when he reaches for it. He thanks her. "I didn't know if you wanted large or small," she says, serving Lewis, "so I brought the same size as Charlie's."

"Same as Charlie's? That's okay. That's great."

She puts down Bernadette's dessert and turns to go. Lewis stops her, a hand on her arm. "So which is it?"

"What?"

"The chocolate milk. Is this the large size or the small?"

"Does it matter?" asks Bernadette.

"What do you mean, *Does it matter?* Of course it matters."

"How?"

He frowns across the table at her. How can she not understand? "Well, if it's small, I'll be thinking I should have ordered the large size."

"You will? What if it's large?"

"Then I'll get full, drinking it too fast, and it'll be my own fault."

"Wow. You can't win."

Lewis stares up at the waitress. "So which is it?"

"It's small," says Carol. She leaves.

"Drat," says Lewis.

"This is small?" says Charlie, holding up his glass. "No wonder I'm always thirsty after I finish."

Silence descends on the table like a dove, but does not stay long. Lewis looks up from his third bite of pie. "So your dad is the Stocking Bandit. That is so weird!"

"He's not the bandit."

"But Steve Metworthy said so."

Charlie frowns, trying to find the right words.

"Shut up, Lewis," says Bernadette.

"No, no. Don't you see? This is a good opportunity." Lewis chews and swallows. "We should put our heads together and hatch a plan."

"Hatch?" says Bernadette.

"Sure, hatch. Isn't that an okay word? You hatch a plan, don't you?"

"You hatch *eggs*," says Bernadette. "If you're a bird."

"A plan to do what?" asks Charlie.

"Well, I was thinking. Your dad is in prison, right? I think that's what Steve said. Maybe we could break him out or something."

Charlie sighs.

"Break him out of prison?" says Bernadette. "Out of *prison*? You know what a prison is, don't you, Lewis? Stone walls, iron bars, wardens with guns, cell mates named Snake and the Exterminator. It's not like a game of frozen tag, where you just touch someone who's frozen and they're free."

"I said break him out *or something.*"

"Something like what?"

Lewis shrugs. "Hey, I'm just talking here, Bernadette."

"I'll say."

"Shut up, you two!" Charlie is surprised at himself. He's really upset. It's fear, mostly. Fear that Dad won't come home tonight. That he'll be convicted. Fear that he really will go to jail, for years and years.

He isn't used to feeling this strongly about—well, about anything. And here he is on the verge of tears. He doesn't want to show his feelings, but it's important for Lewis to understand. "I'll say this once, Lewis. My father is *not* the Stocking Bandit. He's not in jail, so we don't have to break him out. He has a lawyer. He'll be home tonight. The police won't even suspect him anymore when they find the real Stocking Bandit."

"That's it! That's perfect!" Lewis claps his hands together, so loud that Carol and Uriah and the middle-aged man buying a slice of white chocolate cake to take home for his wife's dessert all look over. "That's what we'll do," says Lewis. "*We'll* find the real Stocking Bandit."

The three children stare at one another. Well, to be accurate, Lewis stares at Bernadette and Charlie, Bernadette stares at Lewis and grabs Charlie's hand, and Charlie points his head in the wrong direction, somewhere to the left of where Lewis is sitting.

Charlie takes a bite of his dessert. He's almost done. His bandaged fingers grip the side of his plate, holding it steady. His fork crisscrosses the surface, searching for more.

"Come on, guys," says Lewis. "We'll do it! We'll find the Stocking Bandit!"

Bernadette is skeptical. "How are *we* going to find him? The police might do it, but we sure won't."

Charlie finishes his dessert. How can he eat so neatly without seeing what he's eating has always been beyond Bernadette. He dusts his fingers over the empty plate.

Inside, Charlie feels like a wishbone, pulled in opposite directions. On the one hand, he knows Bernadette is right. The three of them make an unlikely detective team: the Hardy Boys—only one of them is blind!

And suddenly it is night, and Charlie Hardy and his brother Lewis, wearing V-necked sweaters and Windbreakers, find themselves on the outskirts of Bayport, staring up an an old mill. "Gosh," whispers Lewis. "Do you think the crooks are inside?"

"Gosh," Charlie whispers back. "Let's find out. We have to keep quiet, though."

Lewis leads the way. "Careful of the mantrap," he whispers.

"What mantrap?"

"The one right in front of you, near the trip wire."

"What trip wire?"

"The one attached to the big gong."

"What gong?"

Charlie takes a step forward . . .

He knows that Lewis's idea doesn't make any sense. And yet . . . and yet he *wants* to act, to do something to clear Dad's name. He would love to shake his father's hand in front of the cameras, to hear his father's voice thanking him.

"Come on!" says Lewis. "The cops aren't going to look for a new suspect. I saw Captain Davicki on the news. He's got all the evidence he needs. The broken machine. The missing cash. The eyewitnesses. He's found his perp. He's not looking for anyone else."

"Perp?" asks Bernadette.

"Sure, perp. What is it with you guys? Don't you watch TV? *Perp* is police slang for 'perpetrator.' A bad guy."

"So a perp—or a couple of perps—might sit around and hatch a plot. Is that right?"

"Charlie's dad needs our help."

"Yes, but Lewis, how are *we* going to help him?" she asks. "How are we going to do something the police can't do?"

These are Charlie's questions, too. But Lewis may have a point. If the police are sure of Dad's guilt, they won't be looking for the real bandit.

Uriah comes over to their table. Charlie can smell him long before he speaks. "Just wanted to say hi to you folks," he says. "Nice to see you again, Bernadette. Charlie."

"Hi, Uriah. Say, where'd you get the money to eat here?" asks Bernadette.

His smell gets stronger. He's leaning over. "Strangest thing," he says. "The money came to me right out of thin air. Do you want to hear? I'll tell you." Charlie can hear metal grating on the tile floor. Uriah is pulling up a chair. "Happened this afternoon. I was minding my own business, like always."

"Uriah sits outside our apartment building, near the southbound bus stop," Charlie explains to Lewis.

"Yuh. I'm sitting there, rubbing my ankle because of this rich dude poked me with his umbrella, and I look up, and that's when I see it, floating in the fall air like a dream of heaven," says Uriah, revealing an unexpected poetic streak. "I followed the bill—that's what it was, a bill—as it floated down the street. And when the wind dropped, I put down my foot. Not my sore foot, the other one. And there it was. Twenty-dollar bill. I put it in my pocket. I figure it came to me from . . . the graveyard." His voice sinks to a whisper on the last phrase.

Bernadette asks how he figures that.

"Wind was in my face all day," says Uriah. "Blowing off the graveyard. I saw the smoke earlier in the day, blowing from the chimney of the creamery. No, not the creamery. You know, the burning place!" Once again, his voice sinks.

"The crematorium," says Charlie.

"Right. And the smoke blew toward me. I figure they were burning someone who did me harm in this life and wanted to pay me back now he was dead. The guilt money came to me on the wind from the burning of my dead enemy, and it was mine! So I went and bought me some dessert."

The children murmur their agreement. That's what they'd do with the money.

Charlie hears the chair scrape again. Uriah is standing up. "Enjoy your meal, you guys. I'm tired. My bus shelter is calling me."

He walks off, stumbling once. That ankle. Charlie thinks about it.

"Did you *see* that guy?" Lewis sounds like he's just bitten into a lemon. "His hair was . . . *moving*." He shivers.

"I dunno," says Bernadette. "I kind of like old Uriah."

"Did it rain this afternoon?" asks Charlie.

She blinks. "Rain? No. It was sunny. Wasn't it, Lewis?"

"I don't know. Yeah, it was sunny. Why do you want to know, Charlie?"

"Oh, it was something Uriah said. I wondered . . . Do you guys think the money he found has anything to with the Stocking Bandit?"

"I don't know," says Bernadette. "Do you?"

"I hope so."

Lewis tries to pay, but Carol won't take his money. "The old guy took care of your table," she says.

"Whoo-ee!" Lewis whistles. "Maybe I was wrong about him." He runs ahead to help Charlie through the door. Bernadette follows, shaking her head. That Lewis.

The three of them walk up Copernicus together, Charlie on the inside, tapping with his cane against the side of the buildings. They cross Grant Street and keep walking. Huge white buildings on the far side of the street, metal fences on the right.

The shades of evening are drawing in. It's a warm and windy one. Debris swirls around. Newspaper pages and posters blow up against the posts of the cemetery fence and stick there.

"I'll phone home from your place," says Lewis. "My parents want to know before I take the bus so they can stop hitting each other." He laughs self-consciously.

"Look, up ahead!" says Bernadette, pointing.

"It's a cat!" says Lewis.

"It's a dog!" says Bernadette.

"It's Superman?"

"No, Charlie, it really is a dog. In fact, it's Casey."

"Mrs. What's-her-name's missing pet?" says Lewis.

"Yodelschmidt? Yes. Come on, let's see if we can get him for her." She pulls Charlie forward, calling out, "Casey! Casey! Here, boy!"

Casey is a black poodly dog—there is a hint of fox terrier as well—with a broken tail and a rakish expression, possibly because his coat needs a trim, and a fringe of curls hangs over his eyes. One of his floppy ears quirks up when he hears his name. He looks back over his shoulder, sneering.

"Come here, Casey!" calls Bernadette. He doesn't move. She moves forward confidently.

Lewis hangs back. "He's not a biter, is he?" he asks. "I hate nippy little dogs."

"Casey is a sweetie," says Bernadette. "Come on, boy! Come here!"

"Mrs. What's-her-name wants the dog back real bad," says Lewis thoughtfully. "Do you think there's a reward?"

The dog eludes them. Ever caught a dog who didn't want to be caught? Casey disappears through the fence posts and into the cemetery. None of the children can squeeze through after him, and anyway there's no reason to think they'd catch him if they did fit.

The sun is well below the tall apartment towers. It's twilight time. Flickering black shapes dart in and among the trees in the cemetery. Lewis shivers. "I got to get home," he says.

"Come on," says Bernadette. "We'll cross the street at the main gates."

Charlie stands on the corner. Bernadette and Lewis on either side of him. He can feel the curb with the end of his stick. Traffic runs quickly past him on its way north. Somewhere over his head, the traffic light is proclaiming its message. Charlie tries to imagine the message changing from stop to go. He can't.

Bernadette and Lewis shift beside him. They know the light has changed. Charlie gets ready to walk. A second or two he hears the traffic slow down. He leans out from the curb, ready to take his first step.

"Careful!" Bernadette pulls him back by his shirt collar. He can feel the rush of wind as a vehicle races by, crossing the intersection against the light.

"Thanks, Bernie," he says.

Charlie lets her lead him across the road and up the street to his apartment. His father, back from the police station, is having a bath. As far as he can tell, his mom hasn't moved from the kitchen.

Lewis calls home to say he's on his way. His mother tells him not to hurry. His father is bowling. "I'm sorry for your trouble, Mrs. Fairmile," he says on his way out.

She doesn't reply.

Charlie walks Lewis to the door. "Do *you* think Uriah's money has something to do with the Stocking Bandit?"

"We can try and find out," says Lewis.

"Yes." He reaches out to pat his new friend on the back. "Yes, Lewis, we can certainly do that. Thanks."

Lewis blushes.

Bernadette's mom is asleep on the couch with the TV blaring. There's an empty bag of potato chips on the coffee table, ripped open to get at the sour-cream-and-onion-flavored crumbs in the seams of the tinfoil. An empty bottle of rye whiskey lies on its side on the carpet. Mrs. Lyall groans and rolls over slightly, and the channel changes, as if by magic. Bernadette knows it's not magic. The remote is underneath her mother.

She turns the TV off with the button on the set and goes to bed.

Her mom has a restless night, rolling around on the couch, turning the TV on and off. Bernadette is awakened later by a Western, and then again by an infomercial for exercise equipment.

CHAPTER TWO

SCENE 13: *Mrs. Yodelschmidt*

 Charlie wakes up with an idea. No, not quite an idea, a pair of facts that might go together. "How long has Mrs. Yodelschmidt had her fur coat?" he asks his mother at breakfast.

Dad's gone off to work early this morning, to make up for yesterday. Mom's unusually quiet. "Why, I . . . don't know, Charlie," she says. In the background, the radio is playing something sweet and light, a fluffy swirling kind of song for harp.

"She got it sometime in the summer, didn't she?"

"I can't remember. Have you taken your vitamin pill?"

"Yes, Mom. Are fur coats expensive?"

"Oh, yes."

No sun on Charlie's cheek this morning. It's cloudy, but it doesn't feel like it's going to rain. The air isn't heavy enough. "Thousands of dollars?" he asks.

His mother doesn't reply. Has she gone? "Would Mrs. Yo-delschmidt's coat cost thousands of dollars?" he asks in a louder voice.

"Oh, yes, I should think so." His mother hasn't moved a muscle. She sounds tired, uninterested. The music ends. The announcer comes on with the news. Charlie runs his finger-tips over the top of the table. Place mat, toast crumbs, sticky spot from the jam jar. Nothing more to eat. He's done. He wipes his hands on his napkin.

The announcer finishes with the Middle East and the Supreme Court. *"Turning to local news,"* he says, *"the police are still interrogating a man held in connection with the so-called Stocking Bandit series of bank robberies. For more on the story—"*

Mom's sharp intake of breath is louder than the click of the on-off switch on the front of the radio. "I talked to the lawyer last night," she says. "Charlie, there's something I think you should know."

In the silence of the kitchen, Charlie hears his own beating heart.

———————

Alf's big toe is worse this morning. He can hardly walk. He has to use his left foot to work the brake and gas pedals, resulting in an even jerkier bus ride than usual. Charlie asks Bernadette about Mrs. Yodelschmidt's fur coat.

"June," she says. "That's the first time I saw it. Maybe July. I remember because she looked so hot, wearing it. Why?"

"And when was the first Stocking Bandit bank robbery?" he asks.

"I don't remember."

"It was in the summer, too, right? On the radio this morning, they talked about the wave of robberies sweeping across the city this summer."

"Okay, sometime this summer. Why?"

"Well, don't you think it's strange that Mrs. Yodelschmidt gets surprisingly rich at the same time as the Stocking Bandit strikes?"

"Are you saying Mrs. *Yodelschmidt* is the Stocking Bandit?" She laughs. "There are eyewitnesses, Charlie. And the guy was caught on the surveillance camera for a few seconds. I saw the film on TV last night. He's not a short decrepit bent-over old lady in a fur coat. He's a medium-tall guy in a suit."

"Like Dad."

"Yes, like your father. Or lots of other guys. What is with you this morning?"

He doesn't say anything. She shakes his shoulder. "Come

on. What's up? *You* sure aren't. Worried about your dad? I understand. I worry about my dad, too."

The bus jerks to an abrupt stop. Charlie slams into the back of the seat in front of him. Someone falls into Bernadette's lap. "Hi, there, little girl," says a slurred voice. Charlie can smell something strong and nasty.

"Get off!" says Bernadette. There's a slap. "Get off, you big oaf!"

"Sorry. Sorry." The slurred voice fades.

"Mom and I are moving," says Charlie as the bus starts up again.

"What?"

"Mom told me this morning. If Dad goes to trial it will mean tons of publicity. The media will be all over him—and us. His lawyer feels that it'd be better if we moved away. So there's a good chance we'll be moving—probably for good."

"Crap!"

Charlie is shocked. Bernadette never swears.

"Mom talked to her director at work. He's taking a new job in Seattle, and he said she could come with him as an assistant. Someone else in the office has a sister in Winnipeg. Apparently they need social workers there."

"Winnipeg? Seattle? Great steaming mounds of crap! These places are far away, Charlie. They might as well be in Asia."

"That's why I'm feeling a bit grim this morning."

"Crap city!" says Bernadette, with feeling. "No, that isn't big enough. Crap country! Crap continent! Crap world!" Swearing makes her feel better, but not for long and not deep down. It's like scratching poison ivy.

The lady in the seat ahead of theirs turns around with a frown. "Crap world!" says Bernadette again, right in the lady's face. She turns back with a sniff of distaste.

The bus pulls around a stalled car. Horns honk. Bernadette grabs Charlie's arm.

"Who's going to take you to school in Winnipeg?" she bursts out. "Who's going to go with you on the bus in Seattle? What's going to happen to you without me?"

"I don't know."

In a softer voice, almost to herself, she adds, "And what's going to happen to me, without you?"

Charlie explains the timing quietly. "Nothing's official yet," he says. "Dad hasn't been arrested. Not too many people know who he is. The lawyer figures we have a few days before the police will move." He sighs. "Today's Wednesday. If we're going to help Dad, we have to move fast."

"You're talking about Lewis's plan? Finding the real Stocking Bandit?"

"Yes. That's why I asked about Mrs. Yodelschmidt and her fur coat."

"You know she isn't the bandit."

"But she might know where the money is. And if we find the money, we're that much closer to the bandit. Just think, Bernie—if we do find him, then Dad doesn't get arrested."

"And you don't have to move to Winnipeg!"

"Pretty good, huh?"

"Good? It's . . . craptastic!"

"Now you're just being silly."

The bus doors open. A loud female voice calls out. "Take care of my idiot son, Mr. Bus Driver. He forgot his lunch, would you believe it? I ran all the way to the bus stop with it."

And another voice. "Aw, Ma! I said I'm sorry."

Charlie recognizes the voice.

"You now how hard I work to feed you, Lewis? Do you know? You and your father would starve without me."

The bus doors close.

The three of them walk across the school yard together. Lewis is excited. "We're going to do it!" he says. "Find the bandit and save Charlie's father. That's great! I'll come home with you guys this afternoon, and we can start right in! What were you saying about the dog lady, Charlie? Do you think we should follow her?"

"Follow Mrs. Yodelschmidt? Why?"

"Because it's what detectives do. Follow her, and she'll lead us to someone else."

"And then what?" asks Bernadette. "Follow them?"

"Exactly."

When they get to class, Mr. Floyd is sitting in his chair with his feet up on his desk. "Hey there," he says as they come in. "Hi, Charlie. Hi, Bernadette. Hi, Lewis."

He's wearing a T-shirt and yellow pants, thinks Lewis. He knows my name. *My* name.

"You are *so* cool," he says.

"I know," says Mr. Floyd.

Charlie thinks about his father during the national anthem and morning announcements. Hard to imagine Dad in jail. He's not a criminal. Not like the kind of people he thinks of in jail. Drug dealers, murderers, psychopaths. His father in jail—it's ridiculous. It's funny. It should be funny.

It must not happen.

Charlie prides himself on not worrying about things. Because he is already so dependent on others, he makes a point of not trying to control events. This relinquishing control is in fact a kind of control. What you don't care about can't hurt you.

His dad's arrest would be different. Moving away from Bernadette would be different. He cares about them.

Must not happen.

———

First period is language. Mr. Floyd talks about emotions. Sometimes, he says, words can get in the way of meaning. Emotion is direct communication. Anger, loss, horror, desire for revenge . . . these are powerful motivators, he says. They tell you *why* things happen.

Charlie taps along with the teacher, checking what he has written as he goes. The front of his Louis Light 200 displays a running line of braille characters, which he can read and edit.

Someone moves off to the left. Charlie can hear the intake of breath. Rachel.

"I don't understand how that helps with the assignment, sir," she says. "The one about what we didn't do last summer. Because I'm still having trouble."

The class sighs. A lot of teachers would sigh along. Not Mr. Floyd.

"Okay, Rachel, answer this," he says. Charlie can hear encouragement in his voice. He may be smiling, but he's not making fun of her. "You went to camp last summer, right?"

"Uh-huh."

"Why?"

"Why did I—"

"Why did you go to camp?"

"I went," says Rachel, "because my parents told me to."

Some snickers.

"That's not an emotion. Let's try again. How did you *feel* at camp, Rachel?"

"Uh . . . hot," she finally says. "And itchy."

Laughter.

"There were mosquitoes," says Rachel, sounding indignant.

Charlie can hear Bernadette groaning. She doesn't like Rachel very much. A high voice from across the class intones, "I'd hate to be you!"

"How about we try another emotion?" asks Mr. Floyd. "A real one. Come on, people, what do you feel right now—you, in the back row?"

"Me?"

Charlie knows that dark lazy voice. It's Wayne. "You talking to me?" The words seem to crawl out of his mouth reluctantly, like night creatures emerging from a cave into the sunlight.

"Yes, yes. Come on. What do you feel right now?"

Long pause, then . . . "Nothing."

"Nothing?"

Another pause. "Bored, maybe."

Laughter. Mr. Floyd joins in. Charlie can hear Lewis's voice. "Bored. That's us in the back row. Bored!"

"Doesn't anyone feel anything stronger than boredom? All right—let's do it this way. Think back to the summer. Think back, Rachel, and ask yourself what *would have happened* at your camp if you'd felt a strong emotion. Say, if you'd felt . . . angry."

"Angry?"

"Really angry. If you felt really angry at camp, what would you do?"

Dead silence in the class now, for a full nine seconds; then a hoarse, wet spit-filled voice. "I'd burn it down!"

Frank's voice.

The bell rings.

"There you go," says Mr. Floyd. "We'll do some more work later. And Rachel, you can be the first to read your new story."

SCENE 14: *Mr. Underglow*

"Excuse me." A polite PBS accent. A hesitant, tapping walk. Charlie recognizes both. "Do excuse me. Is this Mr. Floyd's room?"

"Who wants to know?" asks Mr. Floyd, with his cool joking style.

"I beg your pardon?"

Bernadette taps Charlie on the back. "It's your EA," she whispers. "The guy with the gold umbrella. Remember him at the O and M? *Help, help. I appear to have fallen over.*"

Charlie smiles. Bernadette's a good mimic.

"My name is Titus Underglow the Third," he says now. "I'm an educational assistant. I'll be working with Charles Fairmile. I would have been here yesterday morning, but I was . . . delayed. I came by in the afternoon, but the principal said Charlie was gone. Is this Mr. Floyd's class?" More tapping as Underglow enters farther into the room.

Some people, thinks Charlie, have a natural smile in their voice. Some people—Adrienne comes to mind—have a natural frown. Every time Mr. Underglow opens his mouth, he sounds like he's patting you on the head. At the O and M, crying for help in the middle of a pile of bodies, he sounded like he was doing everyone a favor by talking.

"I'm Floyd. Do you need Charlie right now, Mr. Underglow?"

"No, thank you. I need your notes, Mr. Floyd, so I can braille them for Charles."

"Braille them?"

"Yes. I need to translate them from print into braille so Charlie can do his homework. Did you not get my memo?"

Bernadette taps Charlie on the back again. "He's still got the umbrella. And he still sounds like a snooty patootie."

"Snooty . . . what?"

"Patootie. Patootie. Snooty Patootie." She starts to fizz, like a shaken can of soda.

"Shhh."

Footsteps approach. Two sets of feet, and one umbrella tip. Charlie smiles up in their direction.

"Hello, Mr. Underglow," he says, rising in his chair, holding out a hand.

"Hello, Charles. It's very nice to see you again." Underglow's hand is smooth. "I'll come and get you here after school, with the textbook volumes you'll need tonight. I'll have the day's assignments brailled up by then. I see you're using a Louis Light 200. Do you want me to translate any notes from yesterday?"

"Yes, please." Charlie takes out the disk and hands it over.

"Well done, you." Charlie can almost feel the hand on his head, patting. "And of course I'll walk you to the parking lot and wait for your parents. Do your parents pick you up, or do you take a special bus?"

"Neither one. I take a city bus. Bernadette goes with me."

"Oh. Oh, yes, Bernadette. I seem to recall her." The voice has changed just slightly. Not quite as warm a pat on the head for Bernadette. "Where is she now?"

"Right here!"

Bernadette's voice sounds loud and harsh in contrast to Mr. Underglow's. "Right here, waving my hand. Yoo-hoo! Remember me?"

Charlie smiles to himself. Bernadette hates to be ignored.

"Ah, hello, Bernadette. I'm Mr. Underglow."

"Yes, I know. The third Mr. Underglow."

A small pause, no bigger than a hiccup. "I'll be working in the little room beside the principal's office. Do you think you'll be able to find that?"

"Can do," says Bernadette. "And if I get lost, I'll ask someone. Now, if you'll excuse me, I have a math assignment to finish. Charlie, we have to solve for x if y is four."

Mr. Floyd chuckles smoothly. "That's it, Bernadette. Keep working. Feel free to check out the class, Mr. Underglow. Yes, Rachel, what is it?"

He strides away. Underglow's tapping fades toward the back of the room.

"Say, where's Gideon?" whispers Bernadette. "He's really late today."

"He really was late yesterday," says Charlie.

Bernadette knows better than to challenge Charlie's internal clock. "I mean he isn't here at all. He doesn't say much, but I miss him." Maybe because she happens to be looking in Frank's direction. The bully is firing snot rockets. He holds his head back and blocks one nostril with his finger, blowing out the other one. Small hard gobs of mucus are flying around him.

He notices her staring, smiles, and turns so that his rocket launcher is aimed in her direction. She shudders and looks away.

So there I was at Camp Silver Birch, and it was wonderful. All July I had just the greatest time. It was like a dream come true. I was the most popular girl there. From the minute I got off the bus I was, like, the queen of the place. You should have seen the way the other girls stared at me. Were they ever envious of the way my clothes fit. No one said my shorts were too snug. No one laughed and called me salami hips.

My cabin was the best one there. The Eagles. We were all the best kids in the camp. The other girls really liked me. None of them made fun of the way I looked, or the way I ate my cereal. Gee, Rachel, they said, what a great way to eat cereal. I never would have thought of doing it that way. And I just smiled and said, Righty.

Did the mosquitoes bite me? They did not. I remember one sunny morning—it never rained in the whole three weeks I was there—when I came up from the lake and the bugs were everywhere! The other girls were slapping and scratching and swearing at the bugs, and their arms and legs swelled up in great big ugly bumps, and I . . . just . . . smiled.

I was such a star. I won all the prizes there were at camp. My campfire started with my first match. I swam all the way across the lake, no problem. Then I swam back. No one had ever done that before. The counselors were really impressed. Everyone in our cabin wanted to be my partner in the canoe race. I picked Stacy, because she was the tallest and prettiest—the one most like me—and we paddled across the lake really really fast, and we were in the lead, and we would have finished first, only Stacy fell headlong into the water as we were near the finish. The *canoe tipped over, and we lost the race. Poor Stacy, she was so wet and so embarrassed. She apologized to me a hundred times, and do you know what I did? I laughed and said, That's okay. I forgave her. And we stayed best friends.*

That's my story of what didn't happen this summer, but it could have and oh I wish it did. Rachel Danowski.

Rachel clears her throat, and sits down. Mr. Floyd thanks her for reading and asks the class if there are any questions or comments. Lewis puts up his hand.

"I'm just a little curious about the . . . salami hips," he says, leaning forward in his desk at the back of the class. "Do you mean the hips are greasy? Or meaty? Or what? I'm confused."

Silence. Rachel has her head down. Adrienne sighs loudly.

Bernadette puts up her hand. "I want to know how Rachel eats cereal," she says.

Gideon doesn't show up all day. Mr. Underglow III takes Charlie downstairs just before the final bell. Bernadette goes to her locker by herself. And stops.

Her heart begins thumping louder.

Bernadette stares at her locker in disgust. Someone has drawn crude stick figures all over it. The figures have lots of curly hair, like hers. Their mouths are open in screams of horror. *AAAAH!* they say in dialogue bubbles, like comic book characters. *AAAAH!*

Frank.

She checks over her shoulder. He's not there. Lockers bang shut up and down the hall. School's over, and no one wants to linger.

Each of the stick figures is incomplete—broken in some way. Two of them are missing legs. One has no arms. One of them is just a head, with lots of curly hair and an open mouth, crying, *AAAAH!*

Bernadette can feel her throat drying. She has to admit it. She's scared. Scared of him.

She looks up and down the corridor. Can't see him.

Charlie is with Mr. Umbrella Underglow. She'll have to go downstairs and help him carry all his books. Meanwhile, what should she do about this? She clenches her hands to stop them from trembling. It's up to her. It's always up to her, and she doesn't know what to do.

She finds herself thinking of Gideon. Why wasn't he at school all day? She swallows.

"What's that?" says what's-her-name, the bimbo. Rachel.

"Graffiti," says Bernadette, closing her locker.

"Oh, my! Oh . . . my!" says Rachel. Her pert little nose scrunches up. Her lips bulge. "That's awful. You should clean that up." She disappears into the crowd.

"Thanks."

Adrienne the frowner walks by with a leather book bag over her shoulder. She stares at Bernadette's locker. "Who would do that?" she asks. "I'd hate to be him."

"Frank, I think," says Bernadette.

Adrienne shakes her head. "Mind you, I'd hate to be you." She strides away.

Bernadette's worry drawer is already full. There's the regular stuff: looking after Charlie at school and her mom at home, and wondering where her dad is. Now there's Charlie's dad, too, and Charlie maybe having to move away.

There's no room in the worry drawer for Frank. And yet, there he is. How can she keep him out? How can she not be worried about Frank? He's stronger, meaner, and interested in hurting her. How can she not be afraid of him?

She grabs her books and hurries downstairs. Inside she sounds like the cartoon figures on her locker. *AAAAH!*

"Now, Charles," says Mr. Underglow, "since we'll be together all year, we should get to know each other better. I know a bit about you. I suppose you want to know more about me."

His voice comes from near Charlie's ear. He must be bending down. The soap smell is very strong.

"My grandfather, Titus Underglow the First, was an important and influential businessman in this city. One-third of all the staplers used in North America came from my grandfather's factory. They called him the Rockefeller of Office Supplies. When Gran got cataracts, Grandpa dedicated a lot of his fortune to charities for the blind. I learned to read braille when I was six, sitting on Gran's knee."

"Um," says Charlie.

"I was Gran's favorite grandchild. I promised her I would spend time helping blind people when I grew up. Do you want to know what I look like? Feel free to touch my face. Gran used to touch my face. She said I had the face of a saint."

"Um," says Charlie.

"Do you have any questions? Any at all? Would you like to know more about staplers, for instance? My gran told me such a lot about staplers. Did you know that the original stapler was made for Louis the Fifteenth of France? Of course it wasn't really perfected until the late nineteenth century. The Underglow patented stapler was the office standard of the 1940s. Any of those old movies, with Rosalind Russell or Ida Lupino working in an office, they're using an Underglow stapler."

"What about Titus Underglow the Second?" asks Charlie.

"Who?"

"Your dad," says Charlie.

"I don't like talking about my daddy," says Mr. Underglow.

There's a knock at the door. Two long and two short. The door opens. "There you are," says Bernadette. "I told you I could find the place. Say, Charlie, you'll never guess what that bully Frank did to my locker."

Mr. Underglow touches Charlie's arm to show that he's talking to him. "You have the disk with today's assignments. PAWS will read it for you at home. You have PAWS, of course?"

"Uh, yes," says Charlie.

"Good. Now, there's a lot to carry. Can you and . . . um, um . . ."

"Bernadette," she says loudly.

"Can the two of you get all those books into your knapsacks?"

Braille texts are much longer than print texts. Charlie's math book takes up most of the shelf space behind Mr. Underglow. Bernadette is prepared for this; she has been carrying braille books home from school since first grade. She loads her knapsack and staggers into it. The canvas straps cut into her shoulders.

"Good-bye, Charles," says Mr. Underglow. "See you tomorrow."

Bernadette makes a point of saying good-bye in a loud voice. Mr. Underglow doesn't reply.

She strides through the halls. Charlie hangs on tight, hustling to keep up. "Mr. Underglow's grandmother went blind," he says. "That's why he's interested in me."

"Well, he sure isn't interested in me, *Charles*." She exaggerates the way Underglow says his name so it comes out *Challs*. "Hey, kid, out of the way!"

Charlie bumps against someone. "Sorry," he says over his shoulder. Bernadette pulls him forward.

"Door." She holds it open. "Stairs. Down." She slows so that he can take the first couple of stairs and get a rhythm going. "Ten more steps," she says, leading quickly.

"Is this the way out?"

"No, silly. It's the way to hell."

"I wonder why Mr. Underglow doesn't want to talk about his dad. Do you think—" Charlie almost stumbles at the bottom. "Hey! That was eleven steps."

"So sue me." She pulls him forward. "Come on. Door. And look—Lewis is waiting for us. He can take some of these books." She pulls him outside.

SCENE 16: *Operation Yodelschmidt*

The apartment lobby is deserted at 3:30 in the afternoon. Wood-paneled walls, an unwashed window, a drooping potted palm, two vinyl couches, and an area rug in muted brown, with several cigarette burns on it. There is a strong smell of cooking. The three children stand near the elevator, which sounds like it is descending.

"All right, Lewis," says Bernadette. "You said you had a plan. Here we are, ready to go. What happens now?"

The smaller boy is sending keen glances all over the lobby. "Now," he says, "we begin . . . *Operation Yodelschmidt*." He reaches into his pants pocket and pulls out a pair of sunglasses. "You two go talk to her. I'll wait here."

"I don't understand," says Bernadette.

Lewis explains. "You and Charlie go up to her apartment. She knows you guys; she'll let you in. Once you're inside, look around. Maybe there's some money lying around, or a black stocking mask. Ask her questions. *Where'd you get the fur coat?* Stuff like that. Get her all worried. When she leaves the apartment, I'll follow her. She'll lead me either to the money or to another contact."

He sounds like the mayor unveiling a scheme to make the city rich.

Bernadette's mouth is open.

"*That's* it?" she says. "That's your plan?"

"Operation Yodelschmidt," he says proudly. "I have the coat and sunglasses." He pats his coat pocket. "Even took the cell phone, so we can stay in touch. Ma will think Pa took it."

"You idiot," she says. "How are you going—"

Lewis shushes her. The elevator doors begin to open. "This could be her now," he says, retreating across the lobby to the window.

Bernadette closes her mouth and pulls Charlie out of the way. Desiree Danton gets off the elevator. "Hey there, Charlie," she says, "How are you?"

"Fine, Desiree."

"Hi, Bernadette. Didn't see you at first. You're too skinny. Standing sideways, you almost disappear. Ha-ha."

This would be an appropriate time to turn on the Bright Smile for Adults, but Bernadette can't quite find the switch. She nods and says nothing.

"Well, kids, I'm off for my afternoon walk. Nice day for a stroll, don'cha think?"

She is wearing a very colorful top, blousy around the shoulders and very tight at the waist. Her pants look like they have been glued on. Her hips swivel when she walks.

The doors close. The elevator wheezes up the shaft.

"What's wrong?" calls Lewis. "You didn't get on the elevator. Aren't you going up to talk to Mrs. Yodelschmidt?"

Bernadette leads Charlie over to where Lewis is standing. The lobby window is too grimy to see through very clearly, but she can make out a blur of traffic and the high fence of the cemetery across the street. It's windy this afternoon. A page of a newspaper blows right into the window, then spins away. A curled greeny-gray leaf plasters itself against the filthy glass and sticks there. "Lewis, wait. Could you explain the Yodelschmidt plan in a bit more detail?"

"What do you mean?"

"Just run over it again. I want to make sure I understand."

He folds his hands on his chest. "You and Charlie go upstairs and question Mrs. Yodelschmidt. You worry her. She comes downstairs to check on her money, or to check with her partner in crime, or whatever, and I follow her."

The elevator rumbles as it descends again. Lewis tenses. This could be her now.

He looks absurd with the sunglasses on, but Bernadette doesn't tell him. "Do you know what Mrs. Yodelschmidt looks like?" she asks.

A long pause. The elevator doors creak open. No one gets off.

"Um . . . no," says Lewis.

"Then how are you going to know it's her? How you going to figure out who to follow?"

Lewis takes off his sunglasses and sticks the end of one earpiece on his mouth to think. "That is a flaw in the plan," he says.

Bernadette punches him in the shoulder. "Come on,

Lewis! This plan has to be good. You haven't thought out the Yodelschmidt angle at all!"

"She's not hard to spot, Lewis. Look for an old lady in a nearly new fur coat," says Charlie, reasonably. "There can't be that many in this building in September."

Lewis is peering through the dirty window. He rubs some of the grime away with his hand, squints to make sure. "Hey. Hey! Look!" He points at the leaf, still stuck to he outside of the glass. "What do you make of *that*?" he says.

"Autumn," says Bernadette. "Happens every year, Lewis."

"Oh yeah?" Lewis's eyes are wide. He runs for the front door to the apartment building. "Autumn, hey?" he calls over his shoulder. "What kind of tree drops those leaves?"

Bernadette takes another look.

"It's . . . money, Charlie," she whispers. "A twenty-dollar bill."

She pulls him across the lobby to the door. As she opens it, the wind hits them. A warm wet wind from the east, smelling of car exhaust and factory chemicals. A few dead leaves cavort in the wind. None of them seems to be currency.

Tough green bushes line the path from the apartment door to the street. Bernadette pushes through, pulling Charlie after her. "Careful," she warns him. He takes small steps on the uneven ground.

Lewis is kneeling in the grass beside the outer wall of the apartment, rooting around the refuse and piles of dead leaves. "I don't see any more bills," he says. He looks up as a leaf, a real one, drifts past him on the breeze, then returns to his prospecting.

"Remember what Uriah told us," says Bernadette. "The wind is coming from the east again. From the cemetery." She peers across the street at the fenced resting place of the city's dead. "Where's the money coming from?" she asks. "Where on earth is it all coming from?"

"Shhh," whispers Charlie. "I hear someone."

They crouch down as the voices start. Two voices. The woman speaks first: "What a good boy you are!" she says. "Yes, you are. A really good boy. Two bundles today. What a good boy you are to carry all that! You will get a treat when we get home. Yes, you will!"

The second voice is a dog's. He gives three sharp high-pitched barks.

The children crawl forward to peer through the bushes. An old lady in a fur coat is walking slowly up the walk with a small poodly dog on a leash. Bernadette touches Lewis's arm and leans over to whisper, "There's Mrs. Yodelschmidt. And Casey. He must have come back."

Mrs. Yodelschmidt keeps talking to the dog. "Yes, a treat. You'll like that, won't you! Cheese and liver, mmm-mmm. Much better than those nasty bones! You can have a treat and Mummy will have a nice long bath to wash off all the nasty dirt."

She doesn't notice the children, but the dog does. He whines and tries to pull away from his mistress. Mrs. Yodelschmidt drags him into the apartment building.

The children consider their next move, kneeling on the dusty gray grass beside the tough shrubs.

"I don't want to go up there if she's having a bath," says Bernadette.

"How long do you think she'll be in the bath?" says Charlie. "Maybe we could go up to see her afterward."

"I can't wait around too long," says Lewis. "I'll have to be getting home in an hour or so. But I do have time for a snack," he adds. "We could go to that Pantry place. After all, we have plenty of money."

Bernadette puts her hand on Charlie's arm. "I know you want to do something," she says. "But I don't think it can happen today."

"Tomorrow," says Charlie. "Okay, you guys? We'll do it tomorrow."

"Okay," says Lewis. He heads down the street. Bernadette pulls Charlie after him.

"Going to order the large-size chocolate milk, Lewis?" she asks.

"You know it."

CHAPTER THREE

SCENE 17: *Junior Again*

The Stocking Bandit wakes up just as the alarm goes off. He kills it at once and slides out of bed with a minimum of fuss, hardly mussing up the covers. He tucks the blanket and top sheet back under the mattress, smooths the pillow, and pulls the spread tight and neat. He tiptoes to his closet and gets dressed for work. The bathroom is empty. He closes the door, shaves quietly, and walks in his socks to the kitchen.

Damn. He wasn't quiet enough. The bandit starts guiltily.

"Sorry, Daddy. I didn't want to wake you."

The old man is sitting on the table, hunched over like a raven, and just as gloomy.

"Guess you were awake anyway, huh, Daddy?"

Nothing.

"Guess so."

He switches on the radio for his father. The old man is a news junkie, not happy unless he's up-to-the-minute. They're talking about a cure for prostate cancer. Boring, thinks the bandit. I'm too young and Daddy's too old.

The bandit is pouring cereal into a bowl. He adds some milk.

The old man is watching. He's always watching.

"Would you like some? I can tell you want some. Would you like me to pour *you* a bowl? Hey, Daddy?"

No answer. But he can hear the old man smacking his toothless old gums. He loves cereal. Always did.

"Trix, Daddy. Fruit-flavored cereal. Remember the TV commercials? Silly rabbit. Trix are for kids!"

Did the old man just snort? In disgust? Who's he fooling? The bandit knows—knows—his father likes Trix cereal. Yesterday there were two empty bowls in the sink when he got home after work.

"Come on, Daddy. I'll get you some. We'll eat breakfast together.

He pours for his father, adds milk, and puts the cereal in front of him.

The old man doesn't even move. The bandit eats in silence as the news switches to an account of the Stocking Bandit investigation. *The police are close to cracking the case. A local man is suspected. Sources close to the investigation say charges are imminent. The so-called Stocking Bandit destroyed at least thirteen automated teller machines in banks this past . . .*

The bandit throws back his head and laughs out loud. It's partly relief. That business with the cab yesterday was a bit too close for comfort. Now the thought of this poor innocent local man is too much. He laughs and laughs. He has gotten away with it again.

He tidies up the dishes before leaving for work. Both cereal bowls are empty. Sly old guy—when did he finish? The bandit can't remember. He rinses the bowls and puts them in the sink. The still and silent old man watches him from the kitchen table.

SCENE 18: *Celebrity*

The bus glides through the morning traffic, making all the green lights, pulling smoothly into the bus stops. Romola, the replacement bus driver (Alf noticed lines of livid red stretching from his infected toe all the way up his leg this morning, and is on his way to Mount Sinai Hospital right now), has an uncanny awareness of traffic flow. She seems to sense just when the delivery van ahead of her is going to stop to unload a shipment, when a suicidal cyclist is going to run a red light in front of her, when a parked car is going to pull into her lane without signaling, when a man on a cell phone is going to make a sudden U-turn because his pregnant wife has just told him she needs ice cream *now,* dammit. No one is drinking coffee without spilling on her route this morning, but they could be. Her bus rides that smoothly.

Roger Fairmile sits between Charlie and Bernadette, making sure they get to school all right. He has all the time in the world today, because he's been suspended from his job at the bank (not fired—they can't fire him until he's convicted).

Bernadette notices a change in her friend's father since yesterday. He hasn't told a joke yet. He sits very still in the seat, and he keeps his head down, as if he doesn't want people looking at him. He has shaved, and he's wearing a suit the way he usually does, but he doesn't look like himself.

She can't help thinking of him on trial, maybe convicted. Charlie moving away and never coming back.

The bus comes to a gentle stop in front of Lewis's building. He has remembered his lunch today. Bernadette introduces him to Charlie's dad.

"Pleased to meet you!" says Lewis. "I saw you on TV last night. The famous 'unidentified man.' You look just like him. Of course you would, wouldn't you—I mean, you *are* him." He laughs self-consciously. "Sorry, I don't mean to gush, but I've never met a celebrity before. Not a *real* celebrity. Last year I met the dwarf from that bowling commercial, but he doesn't count."

Bernadette grabs his arm. "Quiet, Lewis."

"I can't even remember his name. It was at the alley where my pa bowls. The dwarf was doing a promotion. Harry the manager introduced me."

"Shhh!"

"Oh, right. Sorry."

People are turning around. A few rows back, a man stands up to check them out. "Hey, it *is* him," he whispers to his companion. "I recognize him from the suit." His companion stands up, too. They are both tall men with stooped, forward-thrusting heads and heavy jaws like cowcatchers on the front of trains.

The bus glides to a halt at the next stop. A woman across the aisle stands up, holding out a section of the local paper. "This is you, isn't it?" she says. "Would you sign your picture?"

Roger looks upset. "I'm not the Stocking Bandit, you know. I'm innocent."

"You are the guy in the paper, though. The guy on television. Aren't you?"

"Oh, yes. I'm him all right."

"Well, that's good enough." She holds the paper up to his

face. Roger takes a pen from his coat pocket and signs. She squints at the signature. "Richard?"

"Roger."

"Roger. Hey, everyone!" she cries. "This is the guy from the TV. The Stocking Bandit." She checks the paper again. "Roger the Stocking Bandit. You know," she goes on, in a lower voice, "I hate bank machines, too! Last month my bank machine took four hundred dollars from my account without paying me. Then it wouldn't give me back my card. I was so mad! I tell you, Roger, if I'd had an ax with me . . ." she says.

"The bank machine over on First Avenue ate my card, and then changed my PIN number without telling me," says an old man with sweat stains on his bright blue shirt. "I couldn't get into my own account. You wrecked that machine back in July, and I laughed."

"It wasn't me," protests Roger.

Charlie leans over to whisper to Bernadette. "You see what I mean about publicity? It's already started."

"We have *got* to find the real bandit," she says. "We can't have everyone suspecting your dad."

"No." Must not happen, he thinks.

"Where's the ax, Roger?" asks a woman with buckteeth and glasses. "They can't find it. Did you leave it in the cab?"

"I didn't leave it anywhere," says Roger. "I tell you, I'm innocent."

"Sure you are," she says. "And I'm Madonna."

The bus stops smoothly in front of Schuyler Colfax School. Bernadette gets to her feet, pulls Charlie after her. Charlie turns to where his father is sitting and sketches a wave.

"Look," says someone. "Who are the kids? Are they with him? Are they the Stocking Bandit's kids?"

Bernadette hurries Charlie out. Lewis scrambles after them. A wall of people rises around Roger.

On the sidewalk, smelling diesel exhaust as the bus pulls away, Charlie remembers that his dad came with them this morning to meet Mr. Floyd. He asks Bernadette about it.

"I think your dad got distracted," she says.

SCENE 19: *Man in the Moon*

For Bernadette the school day passes like gas: uncomfortable, but not too bad as long as you can keep moving. Worse for others than for you. Poor Rachel doesn't understand fourteen math problems in a row. Someone joggles perfect Paul's arm in science class, and a mild solution of H_2SO_4—sulfuric acid—lands on his desk, and his chair, and his crisp new jeans.

Thick white clouds have been piling up all afternoon, and now, last period, thunder grumbles and wheezes in the distance. Monsieur Noël is trying to tell a joke in French. No one is paying any attention.

"Pssst."

Bernadette glances over. Frank holds up a picture he has just drawn—a crude stick girl with big crazy hair. He points at the picture, and then at her. His face splits in an evil grin. She can see the stud in his tongue. He points again. Yes, it's a picture of her. Bernadette hasn't worried about Frank very much today, partly because Gideon is here. He's wearing a different shirt and shorts, but the same vest. He winks at her.

Monsieur Noël finishes the joke. No one smiles. Wayne, at the back of the class, is actually asleep. Monsieur Noël turns to the blackboard.

"Pssst. Bernadette."

Frank is squashing her picture into a little ball. He lets out one of his *Haw haws*—there's the tongue stud again—and pops the picture into his open mouth.

Bernadette feels nauseated. That's *her* he's crumpling up and eating.

His round face floats across the room toward Bernadette. He chews and chews. He looks like the Man in the Moon. What was that song? *If you believed/they put a man on the moon* . . .

Gideon, observing the whole incident, shakes his head sadly.

The bell rings. Paul leaps to his feet, eager to get home and change his pants. He is careful to hold his knapsack in front of the discolorations.

Frank is having trouble with the mouthful of paper. He makes choking noises. His eyes widen. He tries to swallow, can't. His Adam's apple goes up and down. He gags and thrashes around.

Gideon is right next to him. He stares at the other boy without moving.

Bernadette would like to ignore Frank. Let the bastard choke. But can she? He might actually die. Can she live with that?

Monsieur Noël is gone. The other students are leaving as fast as they can. Charlie is stuffing his Louis Light into his knapsack and feeling around for his cane.

Bernadette has almost decided to step forward and try to help, when Frank finally coughs up the ball of paper. It leaves his mouth like a shell leaving a naval gun, traveling half-way across the room. Frank collapses forward onto his desk, gasping.

Gideon nods slightly, gets up to go.

"Hurry, Bernie." Charlie holds out his free hand. "Mr. Underglow is waiting downstairs. Do you see Lewis?"

"No."

"He must be on his way home. He promised me he'd be in position by four o'clock."

She packs her knapsack and puts his hand on her elbow. "Let's go."

"How are you feeling? You sound funny."

Frank's color starts to return to normal. His eyes are closed.

"I'm okay," she says.

Mr. Underglow talks only to Charlie throughout their meeting, ignoring Bernadette as usual, though he does favor her with a farewell nod.

"He always looks so condescending," she says in the corridor. "Like a game-show host when the poor contestant doesn't know the capital of Mongolia. Not that the host knows either, but he's got the answer on the card."

"His gran thought he had the face of a saint," Charlie says.

"Saint Snooty Patootie, maybe."

It starts to rain as they make their way across the playground to the bus stop. By the time they get off the bus, it's pouring. Bernadette holds her knapsack over her head for protection. Charlie shakes his hair out of his eyes. Raindrops bead on his dark glasses as he follows her to the front door of their building.

"Can you see Lewis?" he asks.

"Nope." She checks up and down the street. "Blond girl at the bus stop, redheaded man in a parked car, Uriah, fat man getting something out of the back of a van; that's about it."

His parents don't leave notes for Charlie, but there's a

message from his dad on the phone. He's gone shopping. He asks Charlie to wait at Bernadette's. "Don't hurry home, son," he says. "I'll come and get you."

Bernadette is taking Charlie's books from her knapsack and stacking them on the kitchen table. "It's pouring rain," she says. "Do you really think Lewis is in position?"

"He said he'd be there by four. Six minutes from now."

"So you want to go ahead?"

"Look, Bernie, if we assume he isn't there, then there's nothing to do. And I want to do something. Drop your stuff at your place, and I'll meet you at the elevator in . . . two minutes."

He hears the front door close behind her. He takes a deep breath. "Be there, Lewis," he whispers.

SCENE 20: *K.C.*

Mrs. Yodelschmidt's apartment smells of dust, dog, and old lady, with a hint of something else that Charlie can't identify. A waxy something, not unpleasant, but not exactly fresh.

"What was it you wanted to see me about, dear?" Her voice is nothing like her name. Yodelschmidt: You think high and loud and warbly, like from the Swiss Alps. Charlie is surprised every time he hears the husky alto.

They're in the living room, sitting on a new-smelling love seat, Charlie and Bernadette and Mrs. Yodelschmidt. Mrs. Yodelschmidt sits between them.

"I don't think you've ever been to my place, have you, Charlie?" she asks. The dog Casey seems to be on her lap. Charlie can hear him panting.

Time to be bold, he thinks. A frontal attack.

"I came for a reason," he says firmly. "I want to ask you about the Stocking Bandit."

"Oh, him." She doesn't react at all. "I know who you mean. He breaks into automatic-teller machines at the bank. They've caught him. I saw it on the news. An unidentified man."

"Are you sure you don't know him?" Charlie attacks again.

"Well, dear, they did call him *unidentified,* and they should know. But of course I may be mistaken. I was flipping through the channels, so I didn't really spend a lot of time staring at him. And I don't see as well as I used to."

"Mrs. Yodelschmidt, the man they've arrested—the unidentified man—is my father."

"You know, that nasty Callaghan woman was talking about your father in the laundry room. Just gossip. We never pay attention to gossip, do we, Casey?"

"Well, the gossip is true, for once. My father is the suspect. And I'd do anything to prove his innocence, Mrs. Yodelschmidt. I'd even accuse . . . you."

Now there's a pause. "I don't understand, Charlie. What would you accuse me of? I didn't attack any cash machines."

Bernadette speaks for the first time. "Your apartment has some beautiful things in it, Mrs. Yodelschmidt."

"Why, thank you, dear."

"That TV set is amazing. How big is it, anyway?"

"Sixty inches, the movers told me. You wouldn't believe how big everything looks. The strongman competitions are my favorite. Have you seen them?"

"And this couch is so soft. It's leather, isn't it? Casey's little doggie bed is leather, too."

"Well, we've been together a long time, Casey and I."

"Yes, everything is new and expensive—except for those pictures on the wall. You should see the pictures, Charlie. Funny old circus posters. 'The Knowledgeable Canine,' they say. Some dog act, I guess."

Casey whines and jumps off her lap onto the floor.

"Why do you keep the posters, Mrs. Yodelschmidt?" asks Bernadette. "Do you like the circus?"

Casey circles around the room. The click of his doggie nails tells Charlie that he's getting closer. "Did you see this dog act, Mrs. Yodelschmidt?" he asks. "Is that why you have the posters? You must have seen it."

Casey is nuzzling Charlie now. His nose is right against Charlie's right hip. He starts to growl and worry at Charlie's pants. Charlie tries to push away the dog, but he won't quit.

The old lady sighs. It sounds like gas leaking from an old barbecue. She reaches across Charlie to grab her dog. "Come on, Casey," she says.

Reluctantly, the dog allows himself to be separated from Charlie's pants.

"What is it, Mrs. Yodelschmidt?" asks Bernadette. "Do you want a Kleenex?"

"I'm fine. I was just remembering . . . You asked if I saw the act? I saw it." She sniffs. "Oh yes, I saw it. Let me see . . . four shows a day, a hundred and fifty days a year for . . . dear me, how many years?" Another sniff. "I probably saw the Knowledgeable Canine about twelve thousand times. Stay, Casey! Leave Charlie alone. He doesn't have any money."

"You were part of the show?" asks Bernadette. What did the old ladies say about Mrs. Yodelschmidt's fur coat? *Not something you'd get in the circus.*

"I spent a lot of my life in one show or another," she says. "Small-time, of course. I don't have any real talent. But I liked animals, and I liked the life. I was a ticket taker for the Pete Robertson Overland Zoo and Circus when I first saw Casey. We were out west somewhere, playing a small town with a German name. Casey was digging through the litter under the stands. He found a ten-dollar bill and was trying to eat it."

Her voice is dreamy. She's reliving the scene, thinks Charlie.

"He looked so funny, with the paper stuck to his nose, licking and pawing and getting nowhere. I gave him some cheese and took the bill from him, and put it in my wallet. When he finished the cheese, he went straight for my wallet pocket. I don't know why. The money must have smelled good to him—maybe it got mixed up with some barbecue sauce or something under the stands. That's when I got the idea for the act. I took Casey back to the trailer and started to train him. It only took a few weeks. Such a simple idea."

When she smiles, her face looks younger. "Pete Robertson liked the acts simple. He wanted the audience to understand the story lines. No mysteries. His whole idea was to have everyone leave the show happy and calm. Pete wasn't handsome, but he had something, all right. He was big, too. Like those strongmen on TV." Her smile broadens.

"What did you and Casey do?" Bernadette prompts her. "For the act."

"Huh? Oh. Simple, like I said. A lady in the audience gets her money stolen. It's in a trick wallet, smells like a doggie bone. The lady screams and carries on. The Knowledgeable Canine goes into the crowd, sniffs out the wallet, chases the thief around the main ring, and brings him to justice. The crowd always applauded when the dog dragged the money from the oversize pocket."

Oho, thinks Charlie.

"And Casey was the Knowledgeable Canine?" says Bernadette. "Oh, of course. I just got it. Knowledgeable Canine—K.C. Get it, Charlie? K.C. is Casey. How did he bring down the thief? He's a little dog."

"Well, it was all part of the act," says Mrs. Yodelschmidt. "The thief helped out. Once or twice we worked a version with a magician who made a wallet disappear. Casey would find the wallet in someone's pocket in the crowd. People didn't like that version as much, though. They got confused. A lady screaming is easier to understand."

Bernadette is staring at one of the old posters. She wonders where Biddeford is. "Why did you stop doing your act?"

She sighs. "Small circuses were always in trouble. Pete went bankrupt. Couldn't pay us. That was years ago now. I drifted for a bit. Came here."

Mrs. Yodelschmidt stirs uncomfortably at Charlie's side.

"And now you're rich." Charlie hasn't spoken in a while. His voice sounds harsh. "Fur coat, leather couch, big TV. Miss Callaghan and Desiree Danton wonder why you stay here."

"But I'm not . . . I mean, not really . . ." Mrs. Yodelschmidt is having trouble with the sentence. "Maybe you children had better go now. I don't feel well."

"Mrs. Yodelschmidt." Charlie stands up. "Where does the money come from?"

Silence.

"This is very important to me, Mrs. Yodelschmidt. I want

to help my father. Are you working with the Stocking Bandit?"

"What? No! I . . . I . . . No."

"Casey finds the money, doesn't he. That's why you stay here instead of moving. We heard you, yesterday, talking to Casey. Rewarding him for finding money. Just the way you did back at the circus. Where does it come from, Mrs. Yodelschmidt? If you don't tell me, I could go to the police. They'll be interested. Where does Casey find the money?"

"I don't *know*," she says vehemently. "We go for walks, and he gets it for me. He's been doing it all summer—stacks of twenty-dollar bills. But as God is my witness, I do not know where the money comes from."

She bursts into tears.

SCENE 20A: *A Quiet Resolution*

"You were very convincing," says Bernadette. She and Charlie are in the elevator, on their way back down to the fifth floor. "Are you really going to tell the police about Mrs. Yodelschmidt?"

He shakes his head. "They wouldn't believe me. We have to find the money ourselves and then use it to find the real bandit. Then the police will let Dad go."

That makes sense to Bernadette, too. "You know, Charlie, she sounded convincing. I don't think she knows where the money comes from."

"I know."

"And yet she really is rich. You should see the TV set—it hangs on the wall like a picture." The elevator slows down. "Say, Charlie, did you notice a weird smell in Mrs. Yodelschmidt's apartment?"

"Yes. Waxy. Like candles, but nastier somehow."

They stop with a jerk. "Here we are. Small step down." The elevator isn't exactly level with the hall.

Charlie's apartment door is open a crack. He can hear his mom's voice from inside. "Roger, darling, it's me," she says. "I was so worried when you told me to come home early. Is there a legal problem? Did you . . . ohhh." Her voice changes. "Oh, Roger! You *naughty* boy! What *are* you holding?"

Charlie grips Bernadette's elbow, pulls her back down the hall toward her apartment.

The TV is on at Bernadette's place. It almost always is. She goes to the kitchen to get them a snack. Charlie says hi to Mrs. Lyall, who returns his greeting but doesn't turn off the set. The springs of the couch make a racket as she moves. "Say, I caught your dad on the news last night, Charlie. What'll you and your mom do while he's in the slammer?"

150

"Mr. Fairmile is innocent!" Bernadette calls from the kitchen.

"This guy on *Jerry Springer* says *he's* innocent, too. Was mowing his neighbor's lawn, he says. I don't believe him." Mrs. Lyall snorts. "He was mowing more than her lawn! He's a liar! All men are liars! If I were you, Charlie, I'd figure on them putting my husband away for ten years." There's a hint of real excitement in her voice as she talks about putting him away.

"I don't have a husband, Mrs. Lyall."

"Huh? Did I say husband? I meant dad." She changes the channel again. "Dad, of course. He's as dangerous as that snake there on the Discovery Channel—jeez, can you see the fangs on him? Hey?"

Charlie, of course, can't see.

"Who wants Pop-Tarts?" calls Bernadette from the kitchen.

Charlie likes watching movies or TV with Bernadette. She's way better than the headphones they give out at movie theaters, with their clinical descriptions of the action. *Wyatt fires at Jesse. Jesse fires back at Wyatt. The rooftop gunman fires at Frank. Jesse falls to his left. Doc fires at the rooftop gunman. The rooftop gunman falls in slow motion, turning a somersault on his way to the ground.*

They watch TV now. Bernadette checks out the living-room window, then comes back to sit beside Charlie. Her mom wields a quick clicker, rotating between *Jerry Springer*, the Discovery Channel, and ESPN, which means that they are watching cheating husbands, killer snakes, and fast cars all at once. Bernadette has to concentrate. "Let's see," she says. "A girl in thigh boots is stomping around the stage yelling at a guy with rippling muscles. Her mouth is open wide enough to see her cavities. . . . Now there's a python with rippling muscles that opens its mouth wide enough to swallow a rat. Yuck! Now cars are whizzing around the track toward us. And more cars. It's fast all right, but so boring you could die. . . . And now the guy with the muscles runs across the stage, and the girl kicks him, and the crowd applauds, and Jerry grimaces at the camera, and there's a commercial about diapers. . . . Hang on while I check the window again."

Charlie hears her footsteps fading away. "Do you see Mrs. Yodelschmidt?"

"Not yet."

Click. Click. Click. The diaper commercial vanishes into space, or cable, or wherever the TV signal comes from. "Now," says Bernadette, "a sunburned woman with veins standing out on her arms picks up the snake with a forked stick. She twirls the stick around and around, like she's eating spaghetti . . . and the cars are still whizzing around and around the track. And now a commercial about runny noses. Wait, now, here's the snake slithering through the grass . . .

and the cars again—whiz whiz. Back to the snake—slither slither. The noses—drip drip. Mom, do we have to watch this? Okay, now they're dragging the bad guy with the muscles offstage, and for some reason the girl in thigh boots is taking off her shirt. The audience goes crazy. The bad guy raises his arm, and we focus on . . . his snake tattoo. What is that smell?"

"Pop-Tarts," says Charlie.

"I have to go to the bathroom," says Mrs. Lyall. "I think it was the race cars, ha-ha-ha." The couch creaks as she gets up.

"Race cars?" Charlie whispers to Bernadette. "What did she mean?"

Bernadette sighs. "I think she's talking about all the . . . whizzing."

Her mom doesn't complain about the constant background whispering. In fact, Bernadette has caught her smiling a few times, enjoying her daughter's descriptions.

"I could never do that," she said once, a few months ago. "What you do for Charlie. Describe things on the TV like that. I could never do it."

"Oh, it's just a knack."

"You do a lot for Charlie, don't you. He'd have a tough time without you."

"I . . . guess so."

"My daughter, spending her life doing things for other people. You're a good kid, missy. I want you to know that. A real good kid."

She'd been drinking, of course. She never said stuff like that when she was sober. But Bernadette can't help her heart from beating a bit faster even now, thinking back.

She makes a quiet resolution: *One of these days, I'm going to do something just for me.*

SCENE 21: *Bogart's Little Brother*

They go to the kitchen to eat their snack. The Pop-Tarts are strawberry. Charlie sits at the table. Bernadette takes hers over to the window. "Raining harder than ever," she says.

"Thunder's coming soon. I can feel it." His skin has been tingling off and on all day. "Good Pop-Tarts," he says.

"I opened a new box. I don't want to think about things with legs when I'm eating."

Mrs. Lyall is still watching TV. The couch creaks as she shifts around.

"Charlie!" Bernadette almost chokes on her mouthful of Pop-Tart. "Charlie, it's happening. Mrs. Yodelschmidt's going for a walk in the rain. Mink coat, Casey, and all. She's heading south. And she's not alone."

Charlie sits up straight. "You mean?"

He can hear the smile in her voice. "There's this strange little guy following her."

"Lewis?"

"Uh-huh."

Charlie holds out his hand. She shakes it. "Operation Yodelschmidt is into phase two."

"Not too many people out and about in the rain. There's a jogger, and a lady with a broken umbrella, and Mrs. Yodelschmidt, and her faithful shadow." She bursts out laughing.

"What?"

"Lewis is so clumsy. He's wearing this trench coat that's way too big for him, and he's got the collar turned up. He looks like Humphrey Bogart's special little brother. And he keeps ducking behind things. Now he's hiding behind a parking meter. What a clown! Good thing she doesn't turn around."

Charlie finishes his Pop-Tart.

"Okay, she's crossing Copernicus Street now. And so is he. He's going to have to hurry. She's on the other side of the street, and the light is changing. He runs after her."

"Come on, Lewis," he mutters.

A flutter against his eyelids. A small gasp from Bernadette.

"Lightning," she says. "A big one, forking down near the waterfront." Thunder follows after a few seconds. Charlie's skin tingles.

"Where are they now?"

"I can't tell. The rain is coming down pretty hard. I think the two of them crossed the street. It's hard to—oooh!"

On the heels of her exclamation is a momentous *thump* of thunder. The storm is right overhead. Charlie jumps. Mrs. Lyall swears.

"The TV's out!" she cries. "There's nothing to watch!"

Nothing to watch. She makes it sound like a form of torture.

Rain hangs in the kitchen window like wet curtains. Bernadette reaches for a Pop-Tart.

Her mom storms in. "Damned television," she says. "Now I'll never find out about those back-fence cheaters." In her tight-fitting sweater suit of deep black with white piping, she looks like a small killer whale.

"Too bad," says Charlie.

Bernadette is still by the window, looking out for Lewis. It's a monsoon outside. Rain sweeps down the street like a scythe. Cars creep by, wipers going hard, red brake lights winking. Thunder booms and rattles overhead.

"Hey, Pop-Tarts! Gimme one!" Cherie takes a big heavy bite. "Ah, I love the taste of jam in my mouth. When I was a kid my mom used to give us spoonfuls of jam to shut us up. Edna, over at the Money Mart, used to do it, too, until her daughter got sick from some past-due stuff. Now she checks the date on everything. Not Edna—her daughter. Strawberry jam, I think it was. Your mom ever feed you jam to shut you up, Charlie?"

"Um . . . no."

"I remember when they invented Pop-Tarts. What does that make me, hey? I'm an original, just like them. Pop-Tarts!" She chews ruminatively, savoring the experience.

Old, thinks Bernadette. It makes you old.

"Pop-Tarts went into space with the astronauts. Think of that! Can't say that about your snacks today. Did Pizza Pops go into space? Or Strawberry Surge Fruit Blasters? Or—"

The phone rings. Bernadette answers. "Hello?" She raises her voice. "Hello? What did you say? There's too much interference. You're *what*?"

She listens hard, the phone against her ear. "It's Lewis," she whispers to Charlie.

"Lewis who?" asks Mom, suddenly alert. "The guy who was here the other night? That Lewis? Bernadette, is he a boyfriend?" Mom has her hands on her hips. "I warn you, missy, you'd better watch yourself. Boys are all the same!"

Bernadette ignores her. "I can't hear you, Lewis. Where are you calling from?"

"The cemetery!" Lewis tries to get as much power as he can behind the whispered words. Stupid cell phone. Stupid thunderstorm. "I'm calling from the middle of the cemetery. I'm following Mrs. Yodelschmidt."

Lightning flashes overhead, and thunder roars right afterward. Lewis shivers with fear and cold.

"What's she doing in the cemetery?"

"Walking her dog. I don't know. I've got to go. I'll call back."

Where'd she go? He runs to a square tomb with a cross on top. He peers around the cross. His glasses are fogged up again. He wipes them on his sleeve.

There she is. A small old lady in a mink coat and dripping plastic hat. She's on the asphalt path, leading north. Lewis follows like a ghost, dodging from tomb to tomb.

They are the only ones in the cemetery during the storm. He's so uncomfortable. He blows his nose on his hand—boy, if Ma could see that!—and shivers. Shadowing people looks way easier on TV.

He nips around the edge of a tombstone with an angel on top and almost falls into a deep rectangular hole with a pile of earth on the other side. He gasps aloud. A newly dug grave, and he almost fell in. What am I doing here?

Another flash of lightning. He scoots around the pile of earth, keeping Mrs. Y in view.

Wait a minute. Mrs. Y has a leash in her hand, but the dog is gone. What has she done? Where's the black poodly dog?

Lewis works his way across the sodden grass to the biggest tomb he can find. It's not really a tomb, it's a family what-do-you-call-it—a vault. There's a line of them here. This one is gray stone, dripping wet in the rain, with pillars in front. It's built on top of a hill. The ground falls away sharply at the back. The September rain pours down.

He peers around a pillar. A locked chain hangs across the front door of the vault. The chain is rusty, but the lock gleams like new.

Mrs. Y is calling her dog. Her husky voice rings out. The mink coat droops from her shoulders like a sigh.

"Come now, Casey! Mommy will give you a treat!"

Lewis steps backward, loses his footing, and grabs at a piece of masonry to steady himself. It breaks like pie crust. He slides down the hill, ending up on his heels with his back to the wall of the vault, halfway down the hill.

Thunder again, but it's farther away. The storm is cycling away from the cemetery, over toward the river and the eastern suburbs.

Lewis hears a rustling in the damp leaves beside him. He feels hot breath on his face. Heart beating like a hammer in his chest, he turns his head—and screams. He leaps back, loses his balance, and slides down the rest of the hill, screaming all the while. There's a hole in the wooden fence running along the top of the cemetery. One of the boards is missing. Lewis runs for that hole faster than Peter Rabbit.

SCENE 23: *Charlie's POV*

Charlie sits at his computer keyboard. Thanks to Mr. Underglow, his braille notes and homework assignments are all on disc, so he can work in print. It's much faster to type one letter than three or four numbers. Right now he's busy with the fantasy assignment. What does he want more than anything else?

To clear Dad. To get him out from under the blanket of suspicion, so that there will be no more detectives, no more laundry-room gossip, no more worrying about arrest. But he couldn't read that story aloud to the class. It's too private, too scary, too close to the bone. The assignment should be about himself, anyway. So Charlie thinks about what he'd like to be able to do. Can he put it into words?

The most exciting thing that didn't happen to me this summer was the discovery of my secret power. I was at the beach with Bernadette, spreading out my towel, and I dropped my sunglasses. Usually I have to fumble around when I drop something, but not today. I just thought about where the glasses were, and stretched out my hand and picked them up in one motion. I knew exactly where they were just by thinking about them. It was so strange.

I smelled sunscreen and frying, heard music and laughter, and, underneath it all, the sound of the waves hitting the sand. I concentrated on the next wave, that one particular hump of water rolling closer. The instant the wave broke on the beach, my mind gave a little jump. I didn't need the sound to know what had happened. I knew before I heard.

How can I describe the power? Knowing without hearing or feeling was like —

A hand on his shoulder. He jumps, startled. Usually he can hear people getting close to him. He must have been concentrating really hard on the story.

"Dad?" he says.

He recognizes the feel of his father's hand. Smells like him, too. But there's more than one person in the room.

"Some friends have come to see you, son," Dad says.

"Hey, Charlie," says Lewis. "How come you were sitting in the dark?"

"Lewis!" says Bernadette. She hits him. Good old Bernie.

"Huh? Oh, yeah, sorry."

"Hi, guys," says Charlie.

"Your friends seem very excited about something," says Dad. "Dinner's in a half hour. I've asked them to stay, but

Lewis here says he has to be getting home. And Mrs. Lyall wants Bernadette back, too."

He leaves.

Lewis's voice sinks to a whisper. "First, can we turn on the overhead light, Charlie? Do you mind? I'm a little creeped out here in the dark. I don't know how you do it."

"Lewis!"

"Ow. That hurt, Bernadette."

Charlie smiles.

Bernadette walks to the door, turns on the light. Charlie knows it's her; he recognizes her step. "Okay, Lewis," she says. "Tell Charlie how you found the solution to our problem."

Lewis talks about following Mrs. Yodelschmidt into the cemetery, hiding behind the big family vault, and then being surprised by Casey.

"Boy, did I scream when the dog came out from under the vault," he says. "I was so scared! There was this beast beside me, breathing hot stinky breath right into my face. I fell down the hill and ran away. At least a two-nightmare experience, I'd say."

"You seem to be having your problems with dogs these days," says Bernadette.

"What happened after that?" asks Charlie.

"Nothing. I ran to Bernadette's place, and then we came here."

"But she said you found the solution. That means you know where the money is coming from. Right?"

"Uh-huh."

"Wait. Are you saying that Mrs. Yodelschmidt is getting her money from the cemetery? That's the mystery location?"

Charlie knows the cemetery well; it's one of his favorite places to walk. A cinder track underfoot, trees and grass and quiet all around. Sometimes he'll go over to a tombstone and, with his fingers, trace out the letters and numbers, births and deaths and epitaphs. The limits of people's lives. FREDDA COLLINS. 1891-1980. A good long time. BELOVED WIFE, MOTHER, GRANDMOTHER.

Or, ROBBIE CUPPLES 1956-1957. Not so good. Not so long. UNTIL WE MEET AGAIN.

Charlie grimaces, remembering Mrs. Yodelschmidt's talk of old boots and bones. What has Casey been up to?

"The money's not somewhere in the cemetery," says Bernadette. "It's in this one particular vault."

"How do you know?"

"Because of what the dog had in his mouth when he came out of the vault," says Lewis. "You won't believe it, Charlie. He was carrying . . . this!"

He's holding something up, Charlie figures.

"Lewis, you idiot!" says Bernadette. "He can't see it. It's a twenty-dollar bill, Charlie."

"Sorry," says Lewis. "I keep forgetting. Yes, it's a twenty. The dog had a mouthful of them. One fell out as he was sniffing me. I grabbed it as I rolled down the hill. See—there's still teeth marks."

He hands the bill to Charlie, who feels it carefully. Different denominations have different patterns of raised dots on them. Charlie can make out the tight triangular pattern of a twenty, as well as a small puncture near one edge of the bill. A tooth mark.

This is evidence. Something tangible. It's a step along the road to keeping his father out of jail. Charlie is moved. He blinks behind the dark glasses. "Thanks, Lewis," he says. "Thanks a lot."

"Well, I wanted Operation Yodelschmidt to be a success."

"And it was. Everything happened the way you said it would. Bernadette and I talked to Mrs. Yodelschmidt, got her all worried, and then you followed her. Bingo!"

"What I don't understand," says Bernadette, "is Mrs. Yodelschmidt. Remember, Charlie: 'As God is my witness, I do not know where the money comes from.' But she does know."

"Not really," says Lewis. "I was right there beside the vault, but she wasn't. She was up the hill, looking around for her dog. I don't think she knows which vault he comes out of."

"Maybe," says Bernadette.

"What I don't understand," says Lewis, sitting on the bed with a squeak of springs, "is how the dog retrieves *money?* I mean, why money? It's not natural for them. You think of dogs chasing sticks, or tennis balls, or birds, or squirrels. Is this a special new breed? Money hounds? I've never heard of them."

"Casey," says Bernadette, "is a Knowledgeable Canine."

Charlie is thinking about what to do next. He's got the beginnings of a plan in his head. There should be time to carry it out if the press conference is on Monday.

"Can you find that vault thing again, Lewis?" he asks.

"Sure. It's right near the top end of the cemetery, by the Valley Road."

"Can you take us there?"

"What's the idea, Charlie?" asks Bernadette. He can feel her gaze.

A digitized version of a once-popular song breaks in on his answer. The bedroom sounds like an office elevator.

"Yuck!" says Bernadette. "What is that awful music? Shut it off!"

"I can't!" says Lewis. "That's Ma's cell phone."

It plays nearly the whole chorus of the song and then stops. Lewis breathes a sigh of relief.

"Who has your mom's phone number?" asks Bernadette.

"I don't know. I don't even know why she has her own phone. Pa never calls her."

Full of roast pork, clean and dry, and wearing pajamas, Charlie sits at the computer scrolling through dialogue boxes. The synthesized PAWS voice resonates in his ear. PAWS stands for Program Action With Speech. It's a screen-reading program Charlie uses to find his way around computer software and the Internet. His fingers hover over the useful keys: INSERT, ALT, J, O, H, and the Function keys. He opens a text dialogue box. *Keyboard help on,* the voice reminds him. "Thanks," he murmurs. He sets the verbosity at "Advanced," and scrolls down. PAWS starts to tell him about aboveground vaults in New Orleans. Fascinating stuff, but it's not what he wants. He tries to skip to the next file, presses the wrong key. *Bottom of the Window,* says PAWS. Charlie tries again. *Button not found,* says PAWS. He types INSERT H to ask for help. *Press F6 to change panes,* PAWS reminds him.

Twenty minutes later he hasn't found what he wants. He's read burial ordinances, brochures from funeral homes, descriptions of tomb construction, and accounts of archaeological digs. All in the same quiet uninflected voice. PAWS does not care about anything. PAWS simply utters.

Bernadette can't stand PAWS. "It's like you're talking to an alien," she says. "Like there's nothing behind that voice. Nothing at all."

Charlie's bedroom door is open. He hears his parents' footsteps and takes off his earphones. "Good night, Charlie," his mom calls from the doorway. "See you in the morning."

His dad comes into the room. Stops. "What are you looking at, son? Vaults?"

"Uh-huh. And burial chambers and mausoleums and crypts. Mostly vaults."

"Ah." Dad never discourages him. "Well, I guess it's a stage you're going through. Good night now." A large warm hand lands on Charlie's shoulder.

"Dad, are you worried about going to jail?"

The hand shifts. "I guess I am. This evening my lawyer was talking about grounds for appeal, in case we lose."

"I don't want you go to jail, Dad." He reaches out to grab his father's hand. "I don't want to have to move to Seattle or Winnipeg."

"Ah, yes. I heard about your mom's plans. Awful cold in Winnipeg, son. But it's a dry cold, they say. You'll hardly feel it. I'll be shivering in a damp jail cell somewhere."

"Don't say that!"

"It was just a joke."

"A bad joke!"

"I guess it was. Well, I make a lot of those."

They laugh carefully together. Roger bends down to kiss the top of Charlie's head. "'Night, son."

Charlie goes back to PAWS. How late are cemeteries open? he asks. He learns about a cemetery in Ireland that hasn't closed in 1,600 years. And about some in California that are never open at all—you need a key and voiceprint to get in. F6, F6, F6.

It's getting late. He starts to yawn. Time to exit. *Good-bye,* says PAWS.

SCENE 24: *Real Junior*

It was always the same. Ever since he could remember. Money, money, money. It was all Daddy cared about, but no matter how much he cared, there was never enough. It's the only difference between us, he said. Talking about the rich side of the family.

Junior didn't know why Daddy didn't get along with Grandma. There was a secret, something in the past, and he knew better than to pry. He smiled all during his visits. He even smiled at the chauffeur and maids. He complimented Grandma. And she ate it up. "You are such a charming little boy," she said. Never forget that charm.

When the chauffeur drove him back to the small apartment on the west side, Daddy would swear and call him names. But Mommy would ask him questions: "What was she wearing?" Or "What did you eat?" Poor Mommy.

He went to work at twelve years old, clearing plates, and they paid him in cash at the back of the kitchen. He held the bills gently, as he'd seen his father do, cradling them in his hands. They felt greasy. He rubbed them against his cheek. They smelled of sweat and leather. He stared at them, trying to understand the attraction. What made them so important? He stared and stared, mesmerizing himself. And then—it was as real as pain—he saw his father's face in the money. There was a number at the corners, a twenty or a ten or a five, but his father's grasping angry narrow nutcracker jaw poked up at him from the center of each and every bill. The old man sneered at him, as if to say, *This isn't enough!* And he cried out, in terror, and flung away the bills, and some of them landed in the stockpot, but most ended up in the garbage compactor.

"You bastard!" says the bandit. "You cheap bastard."

The old man sits on the table, prim and proper in his sealed urn. Still sneering at him. The bandit pours another drink of expensive Scotch. "Tomorrow," he says. "I'll get rid of you tomorrow."

He kept the next week's pay, and the next, and brought the

money home to her. He found that they gave him more money when he smiled and told jokes, so he practiced being funny. And he brought the money to her. They'd always had secrets. She took him out to lunch with money she'd hidden from the old man. She got him the job in the restaurant.

They went shopping together. He wanted to buy her something. "What's the most expensive thing here?" he asked, barely taller than the counter. The store smelled of perfume and spice and polished wood.

"Why, Junior, you shouldn't."

That's her voice. Mommy's voice. He hasn't heard it in years. These days he only hears Daddy's.

"Junior, please."

"The most expensive thing," he repeated, waggling his eyebrows. The salesclerk smiled down at him, reached into a drawer, and pulled out a thin rectangular box lined with tissue paper. And there, inside the box, were the softest, most beautiful things he'd ever felt. His fingertips tingled. He heard his mother's gasp of delight and knew that he must buy them for her. These were what money was for. Not for hoarding and worrying about, but for these beautiful things.

"Forty dollars a pair," said the salesclerk softly.

"Oh, Junior, you can't."

"I'll take . . . three pairs."

It was another little secret from Daddy. Silk stockings.

———

It's late at night. In the living room the TV is the only light. Blue-tinged shadows play on the far wall. The bandit is weeping. He weeps whenever he hears Mommy's voice. He wipes his eyes and finishes his drink.

SCENE 25: *Sleep*

Charlie dreams that he is chasing Casey through the cemetery. Lewis is with him. So are Bernadette and Frank the bully, and Mrs. Yodelschmidt, and Uriah. All of them chasing the little curly-haired dog who knows where the money is. They run faster, faster, faster. Charlie can hear the sound of the dog's panting breath. Then the dog stops running suddenly. Charlie can hear the wind in the leaves overhead. A leaf falls in his hand. Not a maple or an oak. A squared leaf with sharp edges. A bill. He feels for the dots, checking the denomination, and his hands begin to burn. The money is on fire.

The others are crying and cursing around him. He hears his father's voice, raised in a shout of surprise, and then fading away. Uriah cries out that his enemy is being delivered into his hands through the fire. Mrs. Yodelschmidt whimpers. Bernadette is asking Frank if he is all right. Meanwhile, money falls like burning rain. Charlie wakes up feeling hot, hot, hot.

2:43, says the clock in his head. A horrible time of night. He goes to the bathroom for a drink of water, cupping his hands under the tap. Charlie wanders through the hall, kitchen, dining area, living room, the rooms he knows best in the whole world. He enjoys the feel of the polished wood under his bare feet. He lets himself sink toward his dad's favorite chair, the soft one with the rip in the side. He tries not to think about Dad in jail, but he can't help it. That lawyer doesn't care about him. She just wants her name in the news. Does Dad know that? Is that why he's worried? He doesn't belong in prison.

Must not happen.

Charlie is tired. His mind floats like scum on bathwater. Thinking of his dad in prison leads him to another out-of-place character. Out of place in this neighborhood. Hmm.

He rubs his forehead and gradually relaxes into the foam comfort of the chair. Sleep steals across the room, taps him on the shoulder, and welcomes him into the unconscious world.

CHAPTER FOUR

SCENE 26: *Mrs. Ellieff*

 Mr. Floyd walks into the room after first recess with a smile like a chandelier. He holds his hands with the index fingers extended.

"Ayyy!" he says.

"Ayyy!" Most of the class laughs appreciatively.

"We've got time for one summer story before we start our math lesson," says Mr. Floyd. "Who will read? I want someone with a sense of drama, and maybe some pathos."

Bernadette can hear the mutters around her. *Did he say Pathos? What's Pathos? I don't know. What did he say?*

"I thought Pathos was one of the Musketeers," says someone in the back row.

The class laughs some more. Mr. Floyd laughs, too.

"All right, then. Someone who at least knows what *pathos* means." He looks around. Uh-oh, thinks Bernadette. He's going to pick me.

But he points his gun finger at Adrienne and pulls the trigger. Bernadette feels unaccountably disappointed. Doesn't Mr. Floyd think *she* knows what *pathos* means?

At that moment the door bursts open, and a stout, corseted Gorgon staggers into the room. She's upset and angry. Behind the sheen of tears, her eyes are sharp as daggers. They probe the room. "My son is going to starve!" she cries.

Charlie turns around in his desk. "What's going on, Bernie?" he whispers.

"Crazy old lady at the front of the class. She's holding a Superman lunch bag."

"My son," says the old lady, "is going to starve unless he gets this!"

"She looks familiar," says Bernadette.

"Sounds familiar, too," says Charlie.

"He left the house this morning at eight-fifteen. 'Don't forget your lunch,' I told him. 'It's on the counter.' He said he would take it, and I believed him. When I saw the bag still sitting on the counter at nine o'clock, I nearly died. I ran out of the apartment, but the bus had gone! My poor stupid forgetful Lewis! I came to the school. I could not let my boy starve to death. The office sent me up here, but . . . I don't see Lewis. Oh, I don't see him!"

Lewis is deep red. His eyes are closed. "I'm here, Ma," he moans.

His mother raises her eyes to heaven. "Thank God!" she cries. "Thank God I hear his voice. He's going to live. But, Lewis, where are you sitting?" She peers at the back of the class. "Ach! What are you doing there? Only losers and lowlifes sit in the back row. It's because of the pen marks on your arm, isn't it? Isn't it? I told your father to punish you!"

"I want to sit in the back row, Ma!"

"Shh. What do you know about what you want? Now come up here."

"Aw, Ma."

"What? You're too proud to get your lunch from your mother? Lewis, I took the bus to school for you. Four long stops, with perverts leering at me. Now come up here."

Lewis rises very slowly. His mother comes to meet him. She's about the same height he is, and a lot broader and more aggressive. She leans toward him, the jut of her chin aiming right into his face.

"Isn't that nice, Charlie," whispers Bernadette. "She's giving him a hug."

The class lets out a collective sigh.

Mrs. Ellieff steps back. "And *that*"—she slaps her son across the face—"will teach you to forget your lunch. You remind me of your father. Sometimes I think you really are his."

Only Frank laughs now. The rest of the class gasps. Mrs. Ellieff walks out the door, shaking her head. Lewis stares after her, whimpering, while the red mark of her palm blooms in his cheek.

"Ayyy!" says Mr. Floyd, shooting after her with his finger.

SCENE 26A: *Adrienne's Story*

The morning was as dark and dreary as a shovelful of mud, and I was filled with a similarly murky and noisome ennui, when suddenly a trans-formation—nay, a transfiguration—took place as the sun shot in startling splendor from its cloud cover—bursting across the sky like a cannonball fired by the Celestial Gunner.

I was in the scullery at the time, in front of the sink, kippered from the hot water at my elbow and the smoking chimney behind me, and keenly alive to the unfairness of my situation. That, in truth, was the source of my ill temper. A minister's daughter fallen on hard times, I was educated and ambitious, but, alas, so poor. I knew I did not belong in service, but I had no family and no money. Gerald's conversation was the only solace I knew, and he would be going back to Oxford today. He had promised to be true to me, but what was the good of such promises? Gerald was the only son of an earl, and I was . . . a scullery maid! I stared up through the narrow grimed panes of the scullery windows, into the jeweled brightness of the sky, and the forces of melancholy grew like a dark army inside my mind, vanquishing hope. Fate held me in her hand. She would, I felt sure, toss me aside, as she had so many like me. Ah, I was bitter as I stared into the sunlit heavens.

And at that moment the scullery door burst in, and Gerald's clear ringing baritone filled the crowded, smoky room. "Dorothea!" he called. "Dry your poor wrinkled hands and come upstairs at once. A lawyer has arrived from London with marvelous news! Your long-forgotten uncle has died and left you a fortune in his will. A million pounds in funds and a stately home with a deer park. A deer park, Dorothea! Papa dare not raise any obstacle to our marriage now! We can laugh at him and his seventeen generations of family honor, moldering in the grave. Do come, Dorothea!"

And at that moment my melancholy vanished, the evil army put to rout by the sudden appearance of reinforcements on the opposing side, forces of hope and good news. I threw down my sponge, took off my maid's cap, and shook out my long, flowing hair. Then I fairly ran for the door. Gerald was waiting to gather me in his arms. As our eyes met I lost my balance and slipped on the wet floor. I fell awkwardly, skidding so that my head landed in the fireplace. My hair burst into flames; in seconds I was surrounded by a halo of fire. I screamed. Gerald and the other servants rushed to help me, but the fire spread, first to my dress, and then his shirt, and then to the oil lamps on the scullery table. The room became an inferno. We all rushed out, trampling one another as the fire spread like a plague, infecting everything we touched.

*When the gallant firefighters finally quelled the blaze, night had
fallen. The great house was a smoking ruin, and Gerald and his family
were all dead. I was alive by a miracle, but would live the rest of my days
in agony, a burned and disfigured wretch.*

For ten seconds after Adrienne sits down, there is total
silence.

"Well, um, I, um, *liked* it," says Rachel finally. "But I . . .
well . . . I just have . . . have . . ."

"No idea," Bernadette helps her out.

Rachel smiles thankfully. "Yeah. No idea what your story is
about. I mean, you're like so smart and you use such big
words I just like bleep over half of what you say, normally,
but, with this story it's like a total *Uhhh*."

Adrienne frowns at the other girl. "A total . . . *Uhhh?*"

"Oh, yeah. I'm like, 'This morning was dark . . . blah blah
blah . . . Gerald blah blah . . . fortune blah . . . slipped
into the fire . . . blah blah . . . disfigured wretch.' Whatever
that means. You know?"

Adrienne stares around the classroom in disgust. Her
thin, high-bridged nose quivers. Her mouth is pulled down
at the corners. "It's a joke," she says. "Just a joke."

Bernadette turns away to hide a laugh. She stops at the
sight of Charlie's open mouth. He's got an idea. It's as clear
as a cartoon lightbulb over his head.

"What is it?" she whispers.

"So that's why," he whispers.

"Why what?"

"Why it's there," he says.

"What's there?"

"The money. Shh. Tell you later."

SCENE 27: *Cookies*

Early lunch is in full swing by the time Bernadette and Charlie arrive at the cafeteria. Along one long wall, seventh-grade
kids buy drinks and hot dishes through a series of hatches.
Along the opposite wall, dirty windows offer a blurred view of
the playground. In between are rows of big rectangular tables,
mostly full of kids hunched over their food.

Noise and smell are almost tangible. Shouts, laughter, hot
grease, scraping chairs, smoke. Bernadette winces. And then,
sudden as a snuffed candle, the noise stops.

Every head—well over a hundred of them—turns as she
leads Charlie across the room. The tapping of his white cane
sounds loud on the cement floor. A moment ago you could
hardly have heard a jackhammer. It was the same yesterday,
and Tuesday. Evidently, the shock of newness hasn't yet faded.

She places his hand on the back of a chair. He pulls out
the chair, sits down, shrugs out of his knapsack.

A susurration of noise. Whisper whisper: *Is that him? It's him, isn't it? Is it? Isn't it?*

"I wonder what Mom packed for lunch today," says Charlie in an artificially loud voice. He fishes inside his lunch bag. "Oh, good!" He holds up a plastic bag. "Carrots!"

A gasp, somewhere in the middle of the crowd.

Bernadette smiles at Charlie. "Full of vitamin A," she says. "Good for the eyes."

A giggle now, and another. Soon the whole cafeteria is giggling. General conversation resumes, and the noise level rises again.

As the lunch period goes by, a few people come over. Most of the overtures are simple and friendly. One kid offers Charlie a big bag of cookies. "Can you eat these?" he asks. "They're oatmeal."

"Why wouldn't I be able to eat them?" When the kid doesn't answer, Charlie goes on. "I'm blind, that's all. I can eat oatmeal cookies. I can play football. I can fold a napkin into the shape of a boat. I'm really a lot like you."

"Sorry," says the guy.

"That's okay," says Charlie, with his mouth full.

"You can't play football," says Bernadette, when the kid wanders away.

"Shut up."

"I saw you play last year, with that special ball that makes a beeping noise in the air. Remember? You can't catch."

"Shut up and have a cookie."

Lewis wanders by, alone. He sits down beside Charlie, his face as long as a Good Friday service. "They kicked me out of the last row," he says. "Wayne and the other guys. They said I wasn't tough enough." Lewis opens a Tupperware container of cabbage rolls, takes out a packet of pepper and a plastic fork, and digs in.

The crowd of lunchers is thinning out. The hatches are closed. The noise level drops.

"Can they *do* that?" asks Bernadette. "Just kick you out?"

"Oh, sure," says Charlie. "Back-row rebels have a very strict code. After what happened to Lewis this morning . . ."

Lewis hangs his head. "My ma. That was the last straw. They said I was . . . not back-row material. Didn't even say they were sorry. I'll be sitting by the door now, with you guys."

"Have a cookie," says Charlie.

"Can I? Thanks." Charlie can hear the bag crinkle as Lewis hunts around, probably for the biggest one. "Thanks a lot."

"I want you to keep up your strength. You're going to need it later today when you show us the vault. I've got an idea about that, by the way. What was the name?"

"Name?"

"On the vault."

"Which vault?" Spoken around a mouthful of cookie.

"Which vault do you think? Not the one with seventeen generations of earls in it, from Adrienne's story. Casey's vault. Our vault. The one with the money in it. Whose family does it belong to?"

"Oh. I don't know. I was hiding behind it, and then I was running away as fast as I could. Now, I *did* notice the name on one vault nearby. I remember thinking—that's a coincidence. But I can't remember the name now."

"And it wasn't the right name anyway."

"No. Sorry."

Bernadette's attention transfers to a familiar figure entering the cafeteria. She grabs Charlie's arm. "Uh-oh," she says.

Charlie hears, from a distance, heavy adenoidal breathing. An old-time deep-sea diver, mixed perhaps with a hint of Darth Vader. Familiar sounds.

"It's you! *Haw! Haw!*"

The cracked, spittle-filled voice is familiar, too. Frank. Charlie stands up. He doesn't know why. Frank is at least a head taller than he is. He'd be able to pick up Charlie like a doughnut, or a basketball, and dunk him.

Now Charlie can smell dirt and sweat and unwashed clothes over the boiled grease and smoke of the cafeteria. "He's coming toward us, isn't he?"

"Oh, yes."

"Anyone we can ask for help?"

Bernadette looks around the cafeteria. The cafeteria monitor is gone. The doors and hatches are closed. It's the end of grade-seven lunch. No one will be back until the start of next period. "Nope," she says.

SCENE 28: *Really Frank*

"Well, I'm here," says Lewis.

Bernadette stares at him. "That's great. You've got five seconds to grow some biceps." She doesn't know what to do. She'd run if she were alone.

Frank stops in front of them. He towers over them the way a factory towers over a row of townhouses. He's holding the end of a piece of pizza in his hand. He chews openly, revealing the pizza in his mouth. Then he flips the end of the pizza at them, skimming it like a Frisbee. It hits Lewis in the chest. He whimpers.

Frank points at Bernadette with a banana-size forefinger. "You hit me," he says in his curious wet lisping voice.

"Umm," she says.

"In the class. The first day. You hit me."

"Well, you hit Charlie first."

Frank stops a moment, chewing, swallowing. He thinks back. It's a slow process. She can almost see the scene from day before yesterday replaying across his face. Finally, he shakes his head. His holed earlobe flaps back and forth. "Did not."

"You know, he didn't," says Charlie in an undertone.

"Shh," she whispers.

"He never did hit me. He didn't hit you either. He didn't hit anyone."

"Shh."

"You hit him, though," offers Lewis helpfully.

"Shut up, Lewis."

"Just trying to get the facts right."

"Well, you're not helping."

Frank growls. "Get lost."

"Who . . . me?" asks Lewis.

"Yeah. Go."

"But I'm . . . um . . . I'm sort of with them," says Lewis.

As a statement of solidarity, this speech lacks force, but Bernadette recognizes how difficult it was for Lewis to say. It is indeed a heroic gesture he is making.

"Would you like a cookie, Frank?" Lewis holds out the bag.

Frank knocks it away. "Cookies! Haw!" He hawks and spits. Charlie hears it land, which is better than not hearing it land.

"Why don't you run for help, Lewis?" he whispers. "Teacher, principal, someone in authority. I'd go myself, but I wouldn't get very far."

"Hey," says Lewis. "That's a good idea."

He runs off to the left. Charlie can hear his footsteps

briefly on the hard floor. Briefly, because after less than two full seconds a large crash resounds from the direction Lewis started in. A table falling over? Something like that. Then a low moan.

"What happened, Bernie?" he asks.

"Lewis tripped over a chair and fell over."

"Uh-huh."

"He clutched at the table, and it fell on top of him."

"Uh-huh."

"He's buried beneath a lot of cafeteria furniture and appears to be stunned."

"Uh-huh," says Charlie.

"I'm going to hit you," says Frank, with a smile. "I'll smash you. Blind boy, you first. You won't know what hit you. Haw haw haw. Then you, Bernadette."

She shivers. The first time she's heard her name on his lips. She backs away, pulling Charlie with her. "Sorry," she says. "I don't know what to do now."

"We can always yell," he says.

"Who will hear us?" She looks around. "There's no one here. No one!"

And then Mr. Floyd opens the door of the cafeteria and peers in. Saved! Bernadette feels as her world has gotten brighter all of a sudden. "Mr. Floyd!" she calls.

"Ayyy!" He smiles like he's really pleased to see them. "Say, how you doing?"

"Help, Mr. Floyd!" cries Bernadette. "Help us! Please!"

He smiles. "No time. I'm supposed to meet 8A Language Arts. Someone said they were on their way here. You kids have fun now. Bye-eee." He waves and backs away. The cafeteria door swings shut behind him.

Bernadette sighs. Another grown-up has let her down.

Frank steps forward. His left hand is clenched into a fist. She can see the brand marking on the back. She gets ready to duck, and kick him.

And then she hears the tapping on the window. She turns around to see a uniformed window washer swaying gently outside the cafeteria, suspended from the roof in a cradle of belts and ropes. He hangs his squeegee on a bucket and leans forward to open the glass casement from the outside. He wriggles out of the cradle and steps through the window. A faint phrase of choir music comes into the cafeteria from the outside, along with his running shoe and short muscular leg.

"Hey! I know who that is," says Charlie.

Gideon climbs over the sill of the window and drops to the floor of the cafeteria. He's wearing a pair of overalls with his name on it. He closes the window, pats Charlie on the shoulder, winks at Bernadette. He is as calm as if he had just walked into his own living room.

Frank had his hands on his hips. "Who the—" he begins. Gideon interrupts with his name. *"Gideon,"* he says. Frank finishes the question: "—do you think you are?" But Gideon's name sticks in the middle instead of the swearword, so that the whole sentence sounds like "Who the *Gideon* do you think you are?" Gideon smiles.

Frank scowls. "What the—"

"Gideon," says Gideon quickly.

"—is going on?" Frank continues.

"Why, you little—"

"Gideon," says Gideon.

It's like a Ping-Pong game. Bernadette's eyes move back and forth between the little boy and the big one. Gideon is perfectly calm. Frank is getting madder and madder.

"I'm talking to you! Will you answer my—"

"Gideon."

"—ing question, you piece of—"

"Gideon."

"Oh, for—"

"Gideon."

"—'s sake."

His timing is perfect. Charlie laughs, possibly because he can't see Frank. Bernadette is frightened. The big guy is swollen like an overblown balloon.

Now he bursts into violent action. He lunges forward, swinging a fist the size of a baked ham. Gideon turns his head. The fist whistles by. Frank swings with the other fist. Gideon turns his head the other way, and the blow misses again. Frank steps back, glaring murderously, before launching a kick that would, if it landed, send the smaller boy into orbit. Gideon sidesteps the kick, and Frank almost falls.

"What's going on, Bernie?" Charlie asks.

"They're fighting."

Frank tries another punch. Gideon doesn't even seem to move, but the blow misses. Frank is starting to breathe heavily now. Gideon hasn't stopped smiling.

"Should we help?" asks Charlie.

"I wonder."

Frank swings his leg high. His huge booted foot seems to float through the air toward Gideon's head. And now the smaller boy reacts. His hands dart toward the boot, moving too fast for Bernadette to follow. Next thing she knows, Frank's kick has missed, and he is standing awkwardly, off balance. Has he hurt himself?

In Gideon's right hand is a boot. He holds it by the laces. It dangles.

Frank's boot. Frank is standing awkwardly because he has only one boot on. His other foot is covered only in a sock. A blue sock with a single dirty toe peeking through.

Bernadette can't believe what her eyes are telling her. The implication is clear: In the single breathing instant that the boot was in front of his face, Gideon managed to unlace and remove it.

"Wow," says Bernadette.

Gideon is perfectly relaxed. The boot swings back and

forth. Frank shakes his head, steps forward, almost stumbles. He looks down at his foot, then back up at the other boy.

A sigh escapes Frank, then a trickle of air that goes on and on until he seems empty. The sigh is physical and metaphysical. He is still bigger than the three of them put together, but he has shrunk. He is diminished. The god has left him. He checks out his stocking foot again and shakes his head.

Bernadette almost—almost—sympathizes.

"Whew," says Charlie. "What's that smell?"

"You wouldn't believe me if I told you," says Bernadette.

The bell rings. Appropriate, since the fight is over. Frank is inert, without initiative or power. Gideon holds the boot out. Frank accepts it, drops it to the floor, and pushes his foot into it. He doesn't look at Gideon.

The next period is beginning. Grade-eight lunch. One of the cafeteria hatches opens. Donna the monitor peers out. Her red wig is crooked.

"What's going on?" asks Charlie.

"Frank is walking away," says Bernadette.

"That's good," says Charlie.

"I hope you're right." Bernadette has seen too many movies where evil is defeated and then returns for one more go. Sure enough, Frank turns and points at them, opening his mouth to say something mean or threatening. Then he pauses, frowning, distracted by something else. He bends to take off his boot, holds it upside down. A rubber ball falls out of the boot. A colorful, hard extra-bouncy ball, the kind you get in a kid's party grab bag. The ball hits the floor and bounces, ricocheting off the metal table leg. Frank's shoulders slump again. He puts his boot back on and walks slowly away.

From under a mound of fallen furniture, Lewis stirs.

Donna the cafeteria monitor takes one look at him and calls for an ambulance.

"I feel fine," Lewis tells her. "I don't want to go to the hospital."

"Shut up." Donna doesn't want another reprimand for negligence.

SCENE 29: *Mistake*

Bernadette and Charlie are in Mr. Underglow's office, stuffing the braille version of the geography textbook into their knapsacks. The books are stacked on the desk. She takes one volume too many, overbalances, and knocks a desk calendar and stapler to the floor.

"Oops." She bends to pick them up, but Mr. Underglow, dropping to his knees, is there ahead of her. He holds the stapler tenderly, checks its action a couple of times. He breathes a sigh of relief.

"This is a sturdy piece of equipment," he says, getting to

his feet. "Well made. Top-loading mechanism, holds a hundred and five standard staples. Note the movable anvil for stapling and pinning. All steel construction, except for the rubber base." He replaces it on the desk and dusts his knees carefully, pulling up a charcoal gray pant leg to remove some fluff from a sock. Bernadette gapes—she's never seen a man in garters before.

Charlie's head is cocked to one side, the way he does when he listens extra hard. "Mr. Underglow knows all about staplers," he says. "His father owned a company that—"

"Not my father," Mr. Underglow interrupts harshly, his face a mask of shock and shame. "Don't speak of my father. He broke my gran's heart. Lost his money and had to work for other people. My father was a failure. You children may go now. I will see you tomorrow, Charlie."

Bernadette realizes that she is still holding the calendar. It's from a bank. The pictures depict wildlife in improbable attitudes. She puts it back on the desk.

Charlie is very quiet on the way home. They sit together at the back of the bus, balancing their knapsacks on their laps. Bernadette's knapsack is cutting into her thighs. She tries to shift it, but there's no other place to put it. This is not the part of the day she will miss if Charlie moves away.

He breaks out of his reverie as the bus bounces over a pothole.

"I *think* I know who the Stocking Bandit is," he says.

"Is this something to do with Adrienne's story this morning?"

He nods. "I wondered who would think about hiding money in a family burial vault. I wouldn't. You wouldn't. But then we don't have seventeen generations of ancestors, like that guy in her story. Not that we know about anyway."

Bernadette tries to imagine a long line of women like her mom, wearing black underwear and too much makeup, stretching back into the past. A chilling concept.

"So I thought about the bandit maybe hiding something in a vault because it means something to him."

Bernadette does not want to be sidetracked. "Remember, Charlie, we don't even know if the money Lewis found comes from the Stocking Bandit. Maybe it's some other stash. Drug money or something."

"No." Charlie is quick to contradict her. "What kind of bill did Uriah pick out of the air? What did Lewis find? All twenties. Drug dealers use hundreds. Twenties are what you get from bank machines. This is the bandit's money. And it's where it is because the vault is important to him."

"You mean, it belongs to his family." She considers this. "That's why you asked Lewis if he remembered the name on the vault."

The bus stops to let people off. There's a space around

them now. Bernadette dumps her knapsack in the aisle and shifts over to give Charlie room, too. That's better.

"So who is it?" she asks.

"I'm not sure enough to tell you," he says. "I have a suspicion, but I won't know until we see the name. Too bad Lewis is in the hospital. He was going to show us the vault today."

"Not sure enough to tell me. Huh!" says Bernadette. "You sound like a detective in a book. Serve you right if you get run over and die, and your secret dies with you, so that the bandit never comes to justice. Oh, look!" She grabs his arms, leaning over him and his knapsack to stare out the window. "Oh, look! It's Dad. Oh . . . no."

"Huh? Where's your father?"

"It's . . . I thought it was him, but it's not. It's Monsieur Noël, the French teacher, getting a ticket. His car is parked in front of the little bakery with the marzipan wedding cake in the window. There's a police officer writing a ticket right now."

The pull is visceral. She wants to leap off the bus and talk to him, and see him smile at her and call her by name. He looks so much like her father that she wants to cry.

When the bus turns onto Copernicus Street, the sun swings behind the tall towers to the west, putting everything in shadow. The bus stops across the street from the apartment building. Bernadette pulls him after her, shoving the other people aside like a snowplow.

Charlie can feel that she's upset. She always gets upset about her dad. He follows as quickly as he can, apologizing when his cane swings around and hits someone on the sidewalk.

"That's okay, Charlie," says a voice at his knees. A familiar voice.

"Uriah?" Charlie feels disoriented. "Uriah, is that you?" He finds the curb with his cane. "Aren't you usually on the other side of the street?"

"Got moved," says Uriah briefly.

"Charlie." Bernadette tugs on his arm. There's something in her voice. "Charlie, we've got a problem."

Fear—that's the something in her voice. "Bats?" he says. She worries about them getting in her hair.

"I wish it was bats," she says.

Suddenly they are in a cave, smelly and dank, with high-pitched bat screams echoing off the dripping stone. Leathery wings swish and flutter around them, beating the air. Pitch-black.

"All right, I don't wish it was bats," says Bernadette. "But we do have a problem. Frank's across the street."

"That's his name?" asks Uriah. "Frank? He's a big one, hey? He kicked me."

Bernadette swallows. She knew this would happen. And this time Gideon isn't here.

"He's got a hard kick, that Frank," says Uriah. "I get kicked a lot, and I know about kicks. His foot hurt."

Charlie eases his knapsack on his shoulders. "Come on, Bernie. Let's go." He seems to have made up his mind. Bernadette lets herself be dragged forward. He's got a strong grip on her elbow. It feels odd to have him leading the way. Must look odd, too.

He taps to the edge of the curb. Traffic is stopped in front of them. The light is red at the top of the street.

"What are you doing, Charlie?"

"I've had enough of bullies. I've got bigger things to worry about."

He steps out into traffic, waving his cane like a rapier with his right hand, pulling her after him. "Frank!" he shouts. "Frank Sponagle. Don't you dare move!"

Bernadette tries to pull him back, but he's stronger than she is, or more determined. He walks straight. His cane hits against a back bumper. The car pulls forward to give him room. He keeps going, waving his cane. "Are we in the south-bound lanes yet?" he says.

"No. This is dumb, Charlie. Let's go back. Quick!"

He ignores her.

"Careful!" she shouts. "You're about to walk into an SUV."

He swings his cane, hits a silver-gray bumper. The SUV driver honks her horn angrily. "That's the front bumper," says Bernadette. She tries to work out how much time they have before the light changes. "Go to the right."

He walks around the SUV, banging it with his cane. Bernadette follows. The SUV driver rolls down her window. "Watch where you're going!" she snaps.

Bernadette explodes. "He *can't* watch where he's going, you stupid woman!" she shouts, finding a vent for her feelings. "That's a white cane. He's blind. And maybe if your ugly and disgusting vehicle took up less room on the road, we could get around it."

The woman's face bleaches with shock. She looks at Charlie, then lowers her eyes. "It's my husband's," she says, weakly, rolling up her window again.

Charlie keeps going.

"Southbound lanes now," says Bernadette. "And the light has just changed."

He walks straight between two small cars. Traffic should be moving, but everyone seems to be watching them. Bernadette feels like she's onstage. Charlie pulls her across the last lane, bangs his cane against the curb, and steps onto the sidewalk.

"Frank!" he shouts. "Where are you?"

"He's coming toward us now," says Bernadette. She can't decide if she's scared of Frank, or still mad at the SUV driver, or relieved to be off the road. The emotions seem to cancel one another out. She feels numb.

Traffic starts to move behind them.

"Look here, Frank," says Charlie, gesticulating with his cane for emphasis. "You have *got* to leave us alone! You understand?"

Frank is not quite where Charlie is pointing. "Turn a bit to the right," whispers Bernadette. "You're talking to the fire hydrant."

Frank looks confused, like he might be having a stomachache, or a religious experience.

Charlie turns so that he's facing the bigger boy and speaks with great force. "Let's be clear. You're a bully, aren't you, Frank? You pick on little kids."

Saliva glistens on Frank's lips and teeth, but he doesn't spit. He nods, trying to get some words out. He seems to be acting against his own will. "I'm . . ."

"A bully. Yes. You tried to attack us the first morning of school. You drew all over Bernadette's locker. You attacked us again at lunchtime today. And now you're here outside our apartment. It's too much, Frank. I want you to leave us alone!"

Bernadette can't remember seeing him as angry as this. He's usually so calm, you'd hardly think he cared about anything. Now he begins pounding the pavement with his cane.

"Bullies aren't important in my life right now, Frank. My dad might go to prison. I don't have time to be scared of bullies. Sorry. You'll have to find someone else to torment."

"I'm sorry," says Frank.

"Why are you bothering *Bernadette?* She likes you, you fool! No one else does. She thinks you're handsome. Don't you know better than to—*what* did you say?"

"I said sorry, Charlie. Uh, sorry, Bernadette. I was wrong." The words fall from his mouth like reluctant tears. He fights them, but he can't help himself.

"That's what I thought you said." Charlie lowers his cane and points his face in Frank's direction. "So you came to say sorry. Well, well."

"I promised," says Frank. "That's why I'm here."

"Shut up, Charlie!" Bernadette pushes him sideways. Her face feels like a sunset. "What are you doing? You liar! I never said anything about—"

"Didn't you say he was attractive? That he might be attractive if he—"

"I said *shut up.*"

The metal stud in the middle of Frank's forehead looks like a bullet hole. She can't think of anything to say to him, so she pushes Charlie again. He stumbles and almost falls, catching his balance against a lamppost.

"Haw haw haw."

Bernadette is in double shock. First, hearing Frank say he

was sorry, and then hearing Charlie tell him that she . . . she *liked* him! Ridiculous. Disgusting.

"Promised?" says Charlie, clinging to the lamppost. "Promised who, Frank? Do you mean Gideon?"

"Hey!" Frank is staring down the street at the sedan with the guy sitting in the driver's seat. "It's Detective Culverhouse! Hey, Culverhouse!"

The man in the car is youngish and clean-shaven. His hair is the color of tomato soup. He looks away, very embarrassed. Then he starts the car. It takes a while. The engine keeps making grinding noises. Finally it fires.

Frank laughs. "Yeah, that's Culverhouse, all right. I know him from the Fifty-second Precinct. He tried to bust me for petty theft once, but he lost the evidence. Wonder what he's going here?"

The gray late-model sedan pulls out and squeals down the street. Frank points after it. "Maybe he's staking out someone. *Haw haw haw.* Wouldn't that be funny?"

"*Haw haw,*" echoes Bernadette thoughtfully.

The afternoon sun, having swung farther around to the north and west, pops out the other side of the apartment building. The street is bathed in sudden light. Frank walks into it without saying good-bye. Bernadette wants to make one thing clear. "Hey!" she shouts at his broad back. He doesn't turn around. "Hey, Frank! I don't like you! Charlie was joking."

Mistake   201

He turns his head, but not to reply. A stream of saliva hits the pavement. He keeps walking.

SCENE 30: *Separate*

"Well, that was surprising," says Charlie. "I never thought I'd hear Frank say he was sorry to anyone. Wonder what made him change his mind?"

Bernadette doesn't know what to think. Her system is still full of adrenaline. She leads Charlie into the elevator. "I wish you hadn't said I liked him."

They unpack Charlie's textbook, and his dad gives them a snack. Cheese and crackers, and apples cut into little pieces. Charlie phones Lewis and is relieved to find him home and healthy.

"The cafeteria monitor thought it might be a concussion," he says. "But the hospital said no. Actually I'm feeling pretty good. Ma says I can go to school tomorrow."

Hmm, thinks Charlie. "Um . . . tomorrow's Saturday," he says.

"I mean on Monday."

"Sure."

"I'm not concussed."

"Sure."

"Sorry I couldn't come over to the cemetery to show you the vault with the hole in the side," he says. "What am I saying, sorry, I'm not sorry at all. I don't want to relive the horror of the experience. Did I tell you about turning my head and feeling this fetid breath on my own cheek." He laughs nervously. "But listen to me babbling on like this. You're probably sure I'm concussed now. Anyway, I'll take it easy this evening and show you the tomb tomorrow. Will that do? Saturday morning, okay? Nine-thirty, right after *The Fairly Odd-Parents*. You ever see that show? That's a great show."

Charlie can hear his mom's voice in the hall. She's telling Dad something. He's saying okay. She's asking if he's sure it's okay. "Lewis, I have to go now," Charlie says.

"Oh, no!" says Lewis. "I offended you. I didn't mean to. I know you've never seen *The Fairly OddParents*. What I meant was, have you *heard* it?"

Charlie can't help smiling. That Lewis. "Bye," he says. "I'll see you tomorrow morning." He hangs up.

"How's Lewis?" asks Bernadette. "Is he concussed? Brain-damaged?"

"He sounds perfectly normal to me."

Mrs. Fairmile wants Charlie to come clothes shopping with her.

"I don't want to go," he protests. "I don't need any new clothes."

"Yes, you do. Stella at work was talking to her sister in Winnipeg. There's a job opening out there in the new year. I've decided to put in my application as soon as I can."

"What if we don't move?" says Charlie.

He hears her sigh.

Bernadette's chair scrapes along the floor as she pushes it back. "I better go home," she says. "See you tomorrow, Charlie."

His mother waits until she's out the door before going on.

"I know you don't want to move, Charlie. I don't want to move either."

"What if the police find the real bandit?" says Charlie. "And the hidden money? What then? We won't move, and I won't need a new winter coat."

She sighs again and strokes his shoulder. "If we're going to Winnipeg, you'll need a new winter coat, Charlie. And there's a sale on at Sears right now. Come on. Where's your cane?"

Bernadette's apartment is empty. This is Friday—Mom's night to do nothing. Kind of like the rest of the week. Who knows where she is or when she'll be home? Bernadette wanders over to the window and stares down at the cemetery. Somewhere in there is the money. Lewis knows where—if he's not in a coma. If he hasn't forgotten. She thinks about calling him. The two of them could find the money, and tell the cops, and then . . . then maybe Charlie wouldn't have to move.

"Ah, crap." She says it out loud. She carries her knapsack to her bedroom. There's no geography homework today, but she finds herself paging through the atlas, looking for Winnipeg. Canada is a big place.

The quiet starts to get to her, so she turns on the TV for company, but flipping through the channels—Captain Kirk, Oprah, tristate Mazda dealers, Sideshow Bob—is no fun without anyone to describe things to.

Meanwhile, Charlie is missing Bernadette, and not just as someone to talk to. His mom walks with her elbows close to her body, so that it's hard for him to hang on. And she has this habit of jerking her whole arm forward, so that he crashes into her. She apologizes, and then does it again a few minutes later. "Escalator," she says, pulling him forward.

He steps out confidently, expecting to go upward. But this is a down escalator. He stumbles and falls into the rider below him, who smells of an expensive scent and appears to be made of concrete sacks. Hard to tell if it's a man or woman. She—or he—takes Charlie's weight easily and, with no apparent effort, stands him back on his feet. The escalator is still moving down. "Thanks," he says breathlessly.

"Uh-huh."

"Oh, my gosh, I'm so sorry," his mom says, from above

them. "Are you all right, Charlie? I'm sorry. I should have told you which way we were going."

Charlie wonders how long until they get to the bottom of the escalator. He can hear people moving around on the floor below. He readies himself to get off. His right hand tenses on the escalator rail. At the last minute, the weight lifter picks him up like a quart of milk and carries him onto the floor.

"Thanks again," he says.

"Uh-huh." And he—or she—is gone.

"Now, Charlie, the winter coats are this way." His mom puts his hand on her elbow and strides forward. He runs to keep up.

SCENE 31: *Harry*

With dinner just a mustard stain and a memory, Lewis Ellieff and his father are on their way to the bowling alley to get Lewis a part-time job.

The idea came to his father when he realized his son needed a shave. "You've got hairs on your lip. Have you noticed, Lucille? The boy has hairs on his lip!" He banged on the table, making the plates rattle. "When I had hairs on my lip, I knew I was a man, so I got a job. Times were hard, but I got a job, because that's what men did."

He stood up, suddenly, frighteningly decisive. "And you'll get a job, too. At the bowling alley. We'll go tonight. Finish your sausage and come on."

No good for Ma to explain that he wasn't feeling well. Pa snorted in disbelief. "He looks fine. Don't baby him. He's not a baby anymore. Not with hairs on his lip."

"He was in the hospital, you imbecile!"

"Imbecile, hey? Well, even an imbecile can see he's not in the hospital now. So what does that make you! Come on, Lewis."

They walk down to Dundas Street to catch the eastbound bus, a boy and his dad and a zippered canvas bag. Pinewood Lanes is in a strip mall, over by the river. Mr. Ellieff throws open the door and sniffs appreciatively.

"Ahhh. I had a job when I was your age, and look at me today." He strides over to his favorite lane and sits down, unzipping his bowling bag. "Look at me, Lewis!" He grips his son's arm tightly. "Look at me. What do you see?"

"My pa sitting in a chair, putting on his bowling shoes?"

"Success, Lewis. That's what you see." Mr. Ellieff straightens up with a grunt. His bowling shirt is wrinkled, and one of the buttons is missing. "Success because I had a job when I was your age."

Mr. Ellieff's plan is simple. "See that guy giving out the shoes," he says, nodding casually. "Behind the counter there—

don't turn your head, boy. Don't be obvious. Just observe him naturally and unobtrusively." He picks up his ball.

Unobtrusively? Lewis turns his head. "That guy? Uh-huh."

"Watch him. Watch his every move."

"Why?"

"You, my boy, are going to *be* that guy." Mr. Ellieff wiggles his fingers into the holes, stares down the lane, strides forward, and bowls a strike.

The shoe guy doesn't look like a young man on the road to success. Right now he's picking his teeth with the corner of a playing card.

After the first game, they get Cokes. The shoe guy pours them. Mr. Ellieff nudges his son. "You watching?" Lewis nods.

Harry the manager comes over to say hi. He's a bit of a family friend, been over to the apartment a couple of times. As usual, he looks like he's on his way to the disco. His sideburns are combed, his sunglasses and fingernails freshly polished. His belly sticks out, but his fitted shirt is tucked into his too-tight pants. Lewis drinks his Coke. The bump on the back of his head throbs in time with his swallows.

"Thanks, Harry!" Mr. Ellieff slaps the manager's back. "Did you hear, Lewis? Harry says he'll make an opening for you behind the counter. There's work at Pinewood Lanes, son."

"Sure thing," says Harry. He pulls the long points of his collar so that they're even.

"A job'll teach his mother not to baby him."

"Sure will." Harry smiles broadly. "You say hi to your wife for me, Gus. She's a fine woman. Oh, excuse me."

He reaches carefully into his side pocket. His cell phone is ringing.

"Hey!" says Lewis.

"Hello?" says Harry, phone to his ear. "Oh, hi, babe." He winks at Mr. Ellieff. "Not now, babe. I'm with a customer. Sure, that's right. I'll call you back, 'kay?"

"You dog, Harry!" whispers Mr. Ellieff admiringly. "Always with the babes."

"I recognize the song," says Lewis to Harry.

"Sure you do, kid." Harry puts the phone away carefully. "It's a classic. 'Knock Three Times.' Tony Orlando and Dawn."

"Ma's cell phone plays the same song," says Lewis.

Harry freezes.

"What?" cries Mr. Ellieff.

Stupid! thinks Lewis. You are so stupid. "Sorry, Pa." He tries to smile. "I borrowed Ma's cell phone the other day. I didn't think she'd need it."

But his father isn't looking at him. He stares at Harry, his face darkening as it fills with blood. In the sudden charged silence Lewis can hear the rumble of a bowling ball at the other end of the alley, the crash of the pins.

Harry moves casually away from them. Mr. Ellieff's arm

shoots out, grabbing the colorful silk shirt by the bell sleeve. "I didn't even know my wife *had* a cell phone," he says. "Let alone one that plays your song. So, who were you talking to just now? Was it Lucille?" A vein jumps out on Mr. Ellieff's forehead.

"What do you mean?"

"My wife, Harry. The beautiful woman who shares my life. Were you just talking to her on the cell phone?"

"Gus, Gus," he says, smiling nervously. "My old friend. I don't know what to say." He tries to break free, but Mr. Ellieff isn't letting go of the shirt.

"What's that song about, Harry?" he says softly. "It's about an affair, isn't it? 'Knock three times on the ceiling if you want me.' That's right, isn't it?" The forehead vein is pulsing. "So, Harry, are you and Lucille having an affair? Hey, Harry? Hey? You *skunk!*" He pushes the bowling alley manager against his own bar. The shirt rips.

"Pa! No." Lewis takes a step back.

"Go home, Lewis," says his father through clenched teeth. "Go now. I'll be along soon. Don't tell your ma that Harry says hi."

Night is falling by the time Lewis gets back to the apartment. Ma is surprised to see him by himself. "Isn't that just like your father," she says. "Sending you home while he has fun. If he was any *less* selfish, he'd be an egomaniac."

"He and Harry were fighting when I left," says Lewis.

"What? Fighting? Punching each other?"

"Well, yeah."

"What were they fighting about?"

"I really don't know, Ma. They were talking about you."

Her face contorts into a sudden fierce smile. She's angry, but pleased, too. "He'd better not hurt him," she says. "He'd better not!"

Lewis isn't sure which *he* she's talking about.

The phone rings. "You answer," she says. "If it's your father, yell at him."

But it isn't Pa. It's Charlie. "Lewis, we need you," he says. "Can you come over to Bernadette's? The police just arrested my dad."

Ma stalks down the hall toward the bedrooms, slams a door.

"I hope I'm not taking you away from something."

"Nothing much," says Lewis.

He hangs up the phone. Do they want to go into the cemetery in the dark? He shudders. Sounds scary—but staying home might be even scarier.

The blaze of sunset is long gone. The last embers are dying away. The storefronts across Grant Street from Lewis's apartment building are brightly lit from inside. There's an eastbound bus waiting outside his building. The driver lets him on, nods solemnly, pulls into traffic. Her uniform jacket, which she hangs on the back of the driver's seat, sports a black armband.

SCENE 32: *Winnipegonian*

"The police found some new evidence," Charlie explains. "I don't know what the evidence is, or how it ties in to Dad, but it's enough to make a real case. When Mom and I came back from Sears a half hour ago, Dad was gone and a police officer was searching our house. He had a warrant and everything. Mom dumped me here at Bernadette's and took off downtown to the police station."

The three children are in the living room—Charlie and Bernadette on the big green couch, and Lewis in the tattered armchair. Charlie looks determined, perhaps because he's sitting up straight. Bernadette looks distressed, perhaps because she's wearing a torn T-shirt with a grape-juice spill down the front.

"We need your help, Lewis," says Charlie. "We need you to show us the vault tonight. Tomorrow may be too late. If we can find the money tonight and show it to the cops, maybe we can stop them from holding a big press conference tomorrow and turning my dad into an *America's Most Wanted* poster."

"And you into a Winnipeger," mutters Bernadette.

"A what?" asks Lewis.

"Or is it a Winnipegonian?"

"Quiet, Bernadette." Charlie doesn't turn around. His face is still pointed at Lewis in the chair. "Can you do it, Lewis? Can you get us to the right tomb in the dark?"

Lewis shudders. He can't help it. It's the association of ideas. *Tomb* and *dark*. "I can show you the place," he says.

"Thanks," says Charlie. "And thanks for coming over as soon as I called. I was afraid you wouldn't want to."

"Are you kidding? I was happy to get away. My parents are being bigger dorks than usual tonight. Big, even for them. I don't know if it's a full moon, or what."

"When do you think we should leave? It's eight fifty-eight now. Is that too early? It sounds busy outside. I don't want anyone to spot us—"

A huge wet sigh interrupts him. It comes from the kitchen and seems to fill the apartment with fatigue.

"Speaking of parents," says Bernadette. "That's my mom. She's sleeping in the kitchen."

"She's given up her bedroom for Charlie to sleep in?" asks Lewis. "Wow. That's very charitable of her."

"Oh, sure. My mom is a charitable woman. Every waking

moment she's not doing good works is spent in contemplation and prayer."

Bernadette can't help making the mental picture of her mother in a full nun's habit, ladling dinner to the homeless. Sister Cherie. The shabby men and women stumble past, receiving their stew like a benediction. Then Sister notices that the next shabby man in line is Dad. Her face darkens behind the wimple. She grips the ladle firmly, raises it high, and brings it down like the hammer of God on Dad's surprised, uncovered head. He staggers backward, falls heavily. She surveys her handiwork with satisfaction, reaches into the folds of her vestments, and pulls out a pack of cigarettes.

"She's kidding about the prayers, Lewis," whispers Charlie.

"And the good works," says Bernadette. "In fact, Mom is sleeping in the kitchen because she passed out in there, looking for something more to drink."

Charlie gets to his feet. His hands are in his pockets. He might be a very young, very cool CEO addressing a board meeting. "We must remember that it's not enough to find the money," he says. "If we get into the vault and discover a million dollars, that won't prove a thing. We have to link it to the Stocking Bandit, which means we have to identify him. And I think I can." He pauses for effect. "I don't have any proof, but in my mind I'm sure that the Stocking Bandit is Mr. Underglow."

"Underglow!" says Lewis. Wasn't Underglow the name . . .

"*That's* your secret?" says Bernadette, leaning back to look up at Charlie. "Underglow? That's the name you couldn't tell me on the bus?"

"I figured that the sort of guy who would think of hiding money in a family vault might be a guy who *knew* about family vaults because his family was rich. And I remembered about old Uriah getting stabbed in the ankle in front of the cemetery on Tuesday—the day of the robbery—by a guy carrying an umbrella."

"Oh yeah," she says. "Mind you, lots of guys carry umbrellas."

"Not when it's sunny."

"I still don't see why you couldn't tell me this afternoon," she says. "It's not like you thought the Stocking Bandit was someone bizarre and famous, like the mayor, or Steve Metworthy on the news, or Michael Stipe. I don't know why you had to go into your great detective pose."

"Michael Stipe of R.E.M.? Why would he be the Stocking Bandit?" Charlie says.

"I like R.E.M. And they did give a concert here this summer."

"About Underglow," says Lewis.

"You know him," says Charlie. "He works with me in school. Carries an umbrella. Calls me Challs."

"I don't know if it matters," says Lewis, "but I just remembered. Underglow is the name of the vault next door. The
one beside the one with the money."

In the moment of breathing quiet, they can hear
Bernadette's mom laughing in her sleep. "Gotcha," she calls.
"You little . . ." Her words trail away, turn into snores.

SCENE 32A: *Junior's Mommy*

The Stocking Bandit is exalted. He is so excited he cannot
stand it. His heart is thudding. His palms are sweaty. He tapes
Daddy's lid down and wraps him tight in plastic. Then he
rolls the urn in sheets of newsprint, folding the ends underneath so that the package has no loose pieces. Then more
tape. Then a blanket. Then, carefully, he slides the padded
bundle into a leather briefcase. Got to be careful, in case of
an accident.

The Stocking Bandit dresses in black. Black suit and shoes,
black gloves. At the last minute, a sort of gesture, he throws a
black silk stocking into his pocket. Will he wear it? Probably
not. But he likes to have it on him. It seems appropriate,
somehow. A piece of Mommy. It's one of the ones he bought
her, all those years ago. He found them in her top drawer, after she . . . after the accident. The feel of silk, Mommy's silk,

is a way of remembering her. His face softens momentarily, as it always does when he thinks of his mother. She had beauty and grace, and she loved her little Junior. What a waste.

With a pain like a fresh paper cut, he remembers the accident again. It was rush hour on the west side of the city. Daddy was working in a hardware store, and Mommy and Junior were walking home from the market with their arms full. A warm afternoon, sun slanting through the trees. She was tired. He was talking about a girl he'd met in school, and Mommy was tired. Too tired to look both ways. Too tired to notice the fourteen-year-old Chevrolet accelerating the wrong way down the one-way street just as she was crossing with her arms full of grocery bags. The car's age came out at the inquest—same as his own. That's why he remembers it. He can see Mommy's face now, looking back at him. He can hear the gurgling chugging engine, and the horn, and the tortured pig squeal of the brakes. He can see her face, one last time. And then . . .

What a disaster. Witnesses described soup and beans and tomatoes flying through the air like rain. One lady on the other side of the street was hit in the back of the head by a can of beef broth and killed instantly. A jar of peanut butter knocked a paperboy off his bike, and the canvas sack full of evening papers caught around his neck, choking him. Pickled beets—a large container, on special that week—spilled across a newly built front porch, staining a large section of wood dark purple; a can of sardines in tomato sauce broke a third-floor window; and a bag of jalapeños split open and scattered, causing much discomfort to the neighborhood pets over the next few days. Three cars were damaged, one seriously. The driver of the old Chevrolet was charged with careless driving, negligence, and multiple manslaughter.

Junior saw none of it. He heard the witnesses, but their testimony did not register. While the people screamed, and the sirens wailed, he stared at his mother's stockinged foot sticking out from under the front of the Chevrolet, and listened to his own heartbeat, and wondered why the world didn't end.

Cabs cost too much, Daddy said. Take the bus, or walk. Take the boy with you. He can help you carry the groceries home. We don't have enough money to waste on cabs.

In Junior's mind, his mother's death, his father's penny-pinching, and the girl he was talking about, all got mixed up. He's never forgiven his father, and he's never been on a date.

He straps up the briefcase and carries it out the front door. He hopes he can find a cab at this time of night—or morning, rather. The moon is a sickle of straw overhead. The sky is the color and texture of tar.

He walks purposefully to the end of his street and waves his free hand. It'd be easier to take a car, but he doesn't drive. He never has. Not after seeing what a car did to Mommy.

"I think we should go to the cemetery right now," says Charlie. He moves across the living room purposefully, confidently, picking up his cane in the front hall. "Come on, Bernie," he says. "Come on, Lewis. Every minute we take is worse for Dad."

He is a natural leader. Lewis gets to his feet, ready to follow.

"Wait," says Bernadette. "We should prepare better. We should pack."

"We're not going on vacation," says Charlie. "Come on."

"We'll want a flashlight," says Bernadette. "And maybe something to dig with. A shovel or a trowel or something. My mom has a trowel on the balcony. Come back, Charlie. Bring him back, Lewis. Sit down. Let's get organized here."

Boys, she thinks. No idea of planning at all. If it weren't for God telling him what to do, Noah would have prepared for the flood by changing into a bathing suit. Charlie comes back to the couch and sits down, grumbling.

"Can I call home, Bernadette?" asks Lewis.

"Sure. Phone's in the kitchen," she replies, on her way to her bedroom. "Don't step on my mom if you can help it."

Bernadette empties her school knapsack onto her bed. There's a working flashlight in her dresser. She throws it in the knapsack. What else will they need? A second flashlight would be a good idea. Water bottles, maybe. Bandages? Probably not. She brings the knapsack into the living room. Charlie hasn't moved. "Hurry, Bernie," he says.

"I'm hurrying."

She moves to the kitchen doorway. Mom is lying on her back beside the fridge, snoring gently. Lewis stands beside, punching numbers into the phone pad. Bernadette finds a flashlight in the junk drawer, but it needs new batteries. She finds some, but they're the wrong size. She finds some the right size, but the flashlight still won't work. She throws it out and gets three juice boxes in the fridge.

Lewis hangs up the phone. "Still no answer at home," he says.

Bernadette goes to the balcony to get the trowel her mom found in someone's garbage. *Can y'imagine throwing this out? Thing's in perfect shape. Honestly, Bernadette, I think people are crazy.* Of course she'd never used it.

Bernadette stares down at the street and the cemetery. A cool night, with a half-moon half hidden behind patches of low cloud. She wishes the street was quieter so they could slip into the darkened cemetery with no one knowing. Things are busier out there than she'd like. A knot of big kids is raveling and unraveling around a nearby streetlamp. Faint giggles float up to the fifth floor on the cool night air. She turns to go, when a familiar silhouette catches her eye. Instinctively, she crouches down behind her balcony railing.

Charlie and Lewis are talking. "Why do you think Mr. Underglow would hide the money in the tomb *next door* to his?" asks Lewis. "Why not in his own? You'd think he'd want to keep the money in the family."

"Maybe he's not that close to his family," says Charlie. "I know he doesn't like his dad."

Bernadette comes back into the room, sits down in a chair, and addresses the boys calmly. "We've got a problem," she says. "Frank is hanging around outside the building."

Charlie folds his hands in his lap and juts out his chin. "Frank?" he says. "Frank from school? I thought he was different now. I thought he was a changed bully. He said he was sorry and everything."

"He and his gang are spread up and down the sidewalk. A dozen kids anyway. Frank has a huge knife in his hand. I saw it."

Lewis swallows nothing. It's all he's got to swallow at the moment. It's the word *knife*. He recalls the brand mark on the back of Frank's hand.

Bernadette puts her hand on top of Charlie's. "I know time's important," she says. "I know you want to go now. But I really don't think we can. Even if Frank and his gang don't beat us up, they'll follow us, and laugh at us, and we don't want that."

Charlie sighs. "No, we don't."

"Do you want to get rid of them?" says Lewis. "We could call the cops and pretend to be scared little old ladies. Cops love them. 'Oh, please, Officer, take that gang away from the front of my building.' What are you smiling at, Bernadette?"

"Nothing. You do a good impression of a scared little old lady."

"Very funny."

"Will the cops bother?" asks Charlie. "Even with three little old ladies calling in, will they send a patrol car? Teenagers hanging around is not an emergency."

"What do we do, then?" asks Lewis. "It's getting late."

"Nine twenty-five," says Charlie. "Not that late."

"We wait," says Bernadette. "In a few minutes the gang will get bored and move on. Until then we can watch TV or play a game."

"I'll try to phone home again," says Lewis.

"Go ahead," says Bernadette. "I'll get us something to eat and drink."

Traffic moves slowly on the road outside. One long blast on a car horn sounds like a bull moose, gruff and bellowing. It is answered by another car horn in a slightly higher key. A more feminine sound, this one, slightly dissatisfied. The deeper blast echoes its feelings again. So does the higher one. The horns call and answer each other as the two great metal animals search for fulfillment across the lanes of traffic.

SCENE 33A: *Maynard*

Detective Perry sips coffee and watches the interrogation through one-way glass. Roger Fairmile is lawyered up, sitting in a crooked chair at a crooked table next to Madeline Maynard, who is, come to think of it, fairly crooked herself.

No, that's not really fair. Maynard is no more crooked than any successful criminal lawyer with sources in the police department.

At least she's honest about herself. When Steve Metworthy asked her how she got involved in the Stocking Bandit case, she smiled right into his microphone and answered: "I wanted to be on the case. Do you realize it's been six months since I had my picture on the front page?"

Here she is in stiletto heels, a tiny black dress, and sparkle blue eye shadow, chewing bubble gum. She looks like a teenager at her first fancy restaurant. But she's running the interrogation. Captain Davicki may have charm and experience, and a killer piece of evidence, but he can't get a confession.

"The cabdriver remembers you, Roger," he says. "And now we have the weapon, too. It doesn't look good." Davicki's jowls swing back and forth. He's being sympathetic.

Roger swallows. "Maybe if I just told you the truth about what—"

"Quiet," says Maynard. A soprano voice around a big wad of gum.

The logs of the Steady Cab Company showed a two-way trip at the time of the robbery—from the National Bank on Grant Street to Copernicus Street, and then back again. Roger admitted taking a cab *to* the bank that morning, but this trip log had him going home first, then back to work. It was a break in his story—the first so far.

Detective Perry interviewed the cabdriver herself. He remembered the fare getting out of the cab to take a walk in the park and then coming back in a hurry. "Typical suit-and-tie guy. One minute he has all the time in the world, next minute he tells me he's late and step on it."

The driver is a bald, bleary-eyed guy with horn-rims. Perry asked him what park he meant.

"You know, the big one over on Copernicus there, with the fence."

Perry asked him if he meant the cemetery.

"Cemetery? Yeah. With the stones, and the wreaths. Yeah, that's the place."

Shown photographs of six middle-aged white guys, the driver picked Roger. "That's him. I remember the suit. Hey, I bet he wants his ax back."

Calmly, very calmly, Perry asked him what ax he meant.

"The one he had with him when I picked him up. I didn't notice the ax at first, because he was holding it beside him, like a cane or an umbrella. When I saw what it was, I was going to drive on—I mean, an ax?—but then I thought, well, he's got a suit, so he should be okay. I found the ax under the seat that day, when I cleaned up. I stuck it in the trunk in case he called about it. But he never did."

The interview took place this afternoon at five o'clock. Warrants were signed an hour later, and Roger was in custody an hour after that—a little over two hours ago now.

SCENE 34: *Zombie Bait*

The three children sit around the coffee table in Bernadette's living room, eating potato chips and playing Monopoly. Snores resound from the kitchen. Charlie moves his thimble eight spaces and feels with his fingertips. New York Avenue is brailled across the top of the space.

"You owe me sixteen dollars," says Lewis. Charlie riffles through his stack of bills.

Bernadette goes over to the balcony window. "Frank's still out there," she says.

Lewis rolls the dice. He lands on Chance and goes directly to jail.

They've been playing for over an hour. Lewis tries to concentrate so he won't have to think about what's going on back home. He finally got through to Ma, but they could hardly hear each other because of Pa yelling in the background. Lewis told her he was going to be late, and she said that was a good idea. "Better sleep over," she said. "Call tomorrow morning. And remember to brush your teeth. You're not an animal. No matter what your father is!" Then Pa yelled at her to shut up, and she yelled at him to shut up and hung up the phone.

The clock in Charlie's head ticks over: 10:34. He feels around for the table, puts his milk down on it. "I just had a horrible thought," he says.

"I know what you mean," says Lewis. "I get those thoughts, too. Like—what if your room is really a cage? And what if your stuffed animals are really wild beasts? And your toys are really monsters? And—"

He stops.

"Not that kind of thought," says Charlie.

"Stuffed animals?" says Bernadette.

Lewis blushes.

"I meant," says Charlie, "that it's after ten o'clock. What if we can't get into the cemetery? They lock the place up, don't they?"

"Oh, there's another way in," says Lewis quickly, without thinking. "A wooden fence along the top end, with a missing board. I ran out that way yesterday."

The instant the words are out of Lewis's mouth, he is wishing them back in. He does not want to go into the cemetery.

"That's great news," says Charlie. "I was afraid we'd have to climb over."

Lewis gives a sickly smile.

Bernadette moves to the window. "I can't see Frank and his gang anymore," she says.

"Then let's go." Charlie stands up, feeling for his cane.

He's so eager, thinks Lewis. So committed. So fearless. It's like he knows the script already. Lewis can't help thinking of all the horror movies where the two stars and their friend do something dangerous, and the friend gets it. Happens every time. And, he thinks, that one—the third friend—is me. The more he thinks of it, the more convinced he becomes. This is not *The Three Musketeers* after all—it's a teen horror flick. Charlie is tall and handsome, real star material. And he's blind, for crying out loud. They'll never kill him. Bernadette isn't a beauty—not like Rachel, say—but she's smart and determined and Charlie's best friend. She's safe, too. No, thinks Lewis, I'm the third friend. I'm zombie bait. Chunky, funny, expendable me.

Bernadette has her hair in a kind of bunch at the back. Too thick to be a ponytail. She hands out cookies and asks if anyone has to go to the bathroom. Lewis can't believe how calm she is. "Have you thought what we're doing?" he says. "We are breaking into a cemetery and digging under a family vault. Isn't that illegal? Isn't it scary?"

They ignore his question. Bernadette puts on the knapsack. It's like he doesn't matter at all. They've already decided to throw him to the creature from beyond the grave.

"Too bad we've only got one flashlight here," Bernadette says.

"Well, I don't need one," says Charlie.

Just before they go, Bernadette covers her sleeping mother with a blanket.

Bernadette leads Charlie down the hall. "Okay," she says. "Now tell me: *Why* did Underglow do it, Charlie? Why become the Stocking Bandit? He doesn't need money."

Charlie stops when she does. "I dunno," he says. "Maybe he's crazy."

Lewis presses the elevator button. "I think he does need money," he says.

"What do you mean?" asks Bernadette. "He's Titus Underglow the Third. His grandpa invented the paper clip. How can he be poor?"

The elevator is just past the fifth floor when the door opens. "Small step up," she says.

"You can be rich and still want money," says Charlie. "Otherwise no one would get any richer." The elevator moves down with lots of little hitches and stalls, like an old man settling onto a park bench.

"I don't know if he's rich or not," says Lewis. "But he needs money. When he came to class that first time, Wayne and I were spinning dimes. You know the game, you flick the dime with your finger so that it spins around and around. A pretty good game, and no one notices you in the back row." He sighs; he's not in the back row anymore. "Anyway, my dime fell off my desk and rolled across the floor. Underglow picked it up, rubbed it, and put it carefully in his pocket. I watched the whole thing. A dime."

Charlie thinks about the police leading Mr. Underglow away in handcuffs. He thinks about his father walking in the front door, laughing his head off. He thinks about his parents kissing happily. He thinks about his dad taking him and Bernadette for ice cream, and then the three of them coming back to play cards.

Bernadette thinks of Mr. Underglow's knee-length black socks and garters. Maybe he is weird enough to be the bandit.

———

It's cool and slightly dank outside. Lewis's shirt and pants were warm enough this evening at the bowling alley, but he could do with another layer now.

Bernadette stops by a big pine tree on the apartment lawn. A nearby streetlight flickers on and off. It looks like a beacon to Mars, signaling in code. "Oh, no!" she says.

"What is it?" asks Charlie at her elbow. "What do you see?"

"I see letters carved into this tree," says Lewis. "Initials, I guess. They look fresh—see how white the wood is. Looks like 'F.S. and B.L.' Is that right, Bernadette?"

Charlie's face splits into a grin. "'F.S. and B.L.'? Why, that's great. Isn't that great, Bernadette?" He chuckles. "Say, is there a heart around the initials?"

"Shut up, Charlie," mutters Bernadette. "Just shut up." F.S. and B.L., she thinks. Frank Sponagle and Bernadette Lyall. So that's what he was doing with the knife.

Charlie's on her right elbow. She reaches with her left hand and grabs Lewis. "Come on," she says. "You're our leader here. Lead us." She pushes him out into the street. He stumbles and is almost run over by a passing car. Not a good start for the third friend.

Keeping the cemetery fence on his right, he hurries up Copernicus, turning onto the footpath along the top of the cemetery. The fence is wooden now. Charlie and Bernadette follow. She has the flashlight, but it isn't helping either of the boys much. No one speaks.

They say that sailors can feel the loom of the land, even in the darkest night or thickest fog. Lewis can feel the loom of the graves on his right-hand side. He is not overwhelmed by a sense of eternal peace and the nearness of heaven. He shivers.

A sports car roars along the Valley Road down below, blue-toned headlights stabbing the gloom like skewers into raw meat. A stunted tree, twisted and hunched over like a crone in a fairy tale, leaps out of the gloom and disappears again as the car roars away. Lewis remembers the tree. The gap in the fence is nearby.

"Flashlight," he whispers. Bernadette holds it up, revealing the break in the line of painted boards. They squeeze through, one at a time, emerging at the bottom of the hill. The slope is steep and smells like dirt and grass and wet.

"Now where?" asks Charlie.

"Up." The family vaults at the top of the ridge make huge black outlines against the star-dusted sky. Lewis starts up the hill toward the nearest one. The ground is dew-slippery and the grade is steep. He slips and puts out a hand to steady himself. Bernadette leads Charlie, the beam from her flashlight bobbing all over as she struggles to keep her feet.

Charlie does not stumble once.

Lewis nearly dies when he hears the rumbling. It seems to come from the ground itself, a deep creaking sound.

"Listen!" Can you shriek in a whisper? That's what Lewis

sounds like. "Did you hear that? It came from over there."
He points wildly.

"I heard something," says Bernadette. "It's stopped now."

"It sounded like an earthquake!"

"Let's move on," says Charlie.

They climb higher. The vault is built into the hill, like a split-level house on a ravine lot. Lewis stops near the bottom of the foundation.

"This is where the dog came out with the money in his mouth," he whispers.

Bernadette shines her flashlight at the side of the vault. "There's a hole in the dirt by the side of the foundation," she whispers to Charlie. "Very rough edges. It's pretty big: about the size and shape of a beach ball. Casey could fit easily."

"But this is not the Underglow vault," says Charlie.

"I can't remember the name of this one," says Lewis. "Underglow is the next one over."

"You're sure?" Charlie reminds himself suddenly, surprisingly, of his mother.

"Yeah, I'm sure." Lewis leads them to level ground. Bernadette uses the side of the vault to pull herself up to the top. She's aware of the weight of the backpack on her back.

Lights twinkle from apartment buildings in the distance, low-level stars. Bernadette shines her flashlight on the front of the vaults. "Lewis is right, Charlie," she says. "There's Underglow next door. Think of that. All the times we've walked here, and I've never noticed the names until now. This is the . . . *Pater* vault. The place is falling down, Charlie," she goes on. "It doesn't look like anyone has visited here in years. Someone cares about the Underglow vault, though. There's a big wreath in front of it."

"Is it locked?"

"Yes," says Bernadette. Her voice is from farther away. She has moved over to check. "Both of them are. Big padlocks and chains on the front doors."

"Okay, then." Charlie is carefully matter-of-fact. "Let's do what we came to do. Casey found his way under this vault and into Underglow's. Is the hole big enough for one of us to get in, or are we going to have to use that trowel?"

Lewis puts his hand on the other boy's arm. "Aren't you scared?" he asks. "Aren't you scared at all? The ghosts of the Pater family could be haunting this tomb."

"Forget it, Lewis," says Bernadette. "I've known Charlie forever. He doesn't get scared."

"Why not?" Lewis wants to know. "*Why* aren't you scared, Charlie? We're in a cemetery in the dark, and my heart is doing gymnastics—and you look like an ad for a yoga retreat or something."

"Uh-huh. Well, Lewis, you try and work out what makes this cemetery so scary now, and try to put yourself in my position, and you might see why I'm not scared. At least, I'm not scared the way you are. I'm scared, all right. My dad might go to jail for a crime he didn't commit. I'm scared to death about that. Now let's take a look in the hole. Time's wasting."

The hole—a tunnel, really—goes into the hill a little farther than cane's length and then twists to the left at a sharp angle. The flashlight beam doesn't show much. Bernadette and Lewis hunker down on their knees, peering doubtfully.

"I don't see any money," she says. "And I can't tell where the tunnel goes. What about you, Lewis?"

"Me?" Lewis shakes his head.

"How wide are your shoulders? Do you think you could crawl in?" she asks him.

"Me?" Lewis peers ahead in the flashlit gloom. His glasses slide down his nose, and he pushes them up again. "Me?" The prospect of crawling down a tunnel under the rotting remains of dead people is too much for him. It'd be a 365-nightmare situation, at least. "Me?" he says again.

"I could get in." Bernadette is trying to disguise the tremor in her voice. She wants to help her best friend. She doesn't want him to have to move. But she does not—*really* does not—want to go into the tunnel.

Charlie gets down beside them. He balances better than they do, using his cane as a third leg. "Nothing, eh, Bernadette? What about you, Lewis? What do you see?"

"Me?" says Lewis.

A huge bug—a beetle of some kind—flies into the beam of the flashlight at just this moment. The bug makes a deep buzzing sound.

Lewis jumps back with a cry of surprise and terror. The bug sounds like a jet engine taking off. It blunders around, crashing into the flashlight and then Bernadette's face. Bernadette screams, and drops the light.

SCENE 34A: *Madeline*

Roger Fairmile's hair is plastered over his forehead. Through the one-way glass, Perry thinks he looks younger than his age, more vulnerable. Davicki's expanse of pale blue shirt is covered in dark stains. Madeline Maynard isn't sweating a drop. She must roll antiperspirant all over herself before climbing into that dress.

Roger is explaining—again—about finding the cab in front of the cemetery gates.

"But, Roger, that's so unlikely," says Davicki. "You're saying the Stocking Bandit got out of the cab, and you got in, and the driver didn't notice the difference between you? The bandit hid the ax under the front seat, but the driver thought it was yours?" Davicki smiles his yellow smile. "The ax had the name of the store stamped on it. The place where you bought it, you know. Solarski Hardware. Do you know the west side of town?"

"Don't answer that." Madeline Maynard fishes in her little beaded purse for an envelope, spits her gum into it, seals it up, and puts it back in her purse.

"Come on, Roger, admit it. It's your ax. You bought it, hid it in the cab on your way home from the bank. Then you hid the money. And then you went back to work." Davicki wipes his forehead on his sleeve. "There. Isn't that a better story, Roger? No coincidences. It's all cause and effect."

He puts a fatherly hand on the younger man's shoulder. "Where'd you hide the money, Roger? In your apartment? If you did, we'll find it."

"Don't touch my client," says Maynard.

SCENE 35: *Charlie's POV Again*

The tunnel fits tight around the shoulders, like one of the too-small winter coats he tried on earlier this evening. Charlie twists himself sideways to work his way forward. He's been crawling for six minutes now. He is alone underground, focused on the sound and smell and feel of moist earth, the soft rustling of his clothes against the sides of the tunnel, and the sharp tang in his nostrils. The soil is fine, with lots of clay in it. Bits of stone, too. It's hard to wriggle through. He's not as small as Mrs. Yodelschmidt's dog.

In a way it's right that he's the one down here, scrambling like a mole. Yes, the job would be easier for a sighted person with a flashlight, but they're in the cemetery because of Charlie. His dad is the one on his way to jail. It's fitting that the flashlight broke, leaving them with no options except to go home, or for Charlie to go in.

He thinks about poor Bernadette and Lewis, surrounded by death and darkness, scared of the horrors that lurk beyond the edge of vision. Poor, sighted people.

Wait a minute. What's that? That's not soil under his fingers. It's moving. Crawling over his hand, up his wrist. Not a worm—not slimy enough. This is a dry and active crawling—a bug. He shakes it off. There's another one. He shakes it off. And another. He makes a fist, squeezing tight. Something cracks under his fingers. Bugs. More than one. Yuck.

Keep going. Got to keep going. Think about Dad in prison. Bugs would be the least of his problems. Charlie pulls himself along the ground. He should be past the first vault by now, getting close to the dead Underglows. If he's been going straight, that is. He reaches forward, grabs two handfuls of earth, and pulls himself along. He does it again. And again. His arm muscles ache. Sweat drips into his eyes. Keep going.

The ground gets wetter. The smell gets . . . *earthier,* if that's possible. He reaches again, and this time his outstretched hands hit a wall of packed earth that stretches right across the tunnel front. He sweeps his hands to the left and right. More dirt, and some concrete shards—heavy stuff with crumbling edges. Charlie can't go any farther. No buried pile of money, no way forward into the vault.

The tunnel is a dead end. What now?

Charlie doesn't think about giving up. He's committed: heart, mind, spirit. He's not backing down this slimy dirty hole with empty hands. So, what's his next move?

He starts when something small lands on the back of his neck. Another bug—must have dropped from the roof of the tunnel. He reaches up to brush it away, but the tunnel is narrow, and by the time he works his arm around, the bug is down the back of his shirt. Oh, well. He tries to ignore the tickling. Come on, he tells himself. Casey came out of here with money in his mouth. If he can do it, you can do it. He may be a Knowledgeable Canine, but you're a determined boy. Think. Think.

"Ouch!" A burning pain in his back. The bug is stinging him. "Ouch!" He cries out again and wriggles frantically. He can't reach around to crush the bug. The burning pain moves down his back. The bug keeps on stinging him. He screams, rolling around, scraping himself against the walls of the tunnel, until he succeeds in crushing the insect and stopping the pain. (Next day there is a vivid aching line, narrow and straight as the scar of a lash, stretching from Charlie's left shoulder blade almost to his waist.) The sound of his voice runs away from him, reverberating farther off.

Wait a minute, he thinks. Reverberating . . . where?

Charlie focuses his mind. Where is the sound going, if the tunnel is a dead end? Where, come to think of it, is the air coming from: It's too fresh for a dead-end tunnel.

Only one answer. Cautiously, Charlie reaches . . . up.

Damp stone. This is the underside of the foundation—the bottom of the vault floor. Charlie's hands play along the underside of the stone until he comes to a sharp edge. And beyond the edge is space. A hole. Charlie crab-crawls forward and reaches up again. Yes. A good-size hole in the floor of the vault. That's the air supply, and a space for his voice to echo.

He struggles into a seated position and reaches one hand into the Underglow vault.

After losing sight of Charlie around the first bend, Lewis and Bernadette walk up and down in front of the hole. Bernadette is holding Charlie's white cane in the middle, like a majorette's baton. She keeps stumbling over roots. The older trees creak in the wind. She tries to avoid feeling too guilty or relieved—guilty about Charlie burrowing under ground on his own, relieved that she's not in there herself.

"What time is it, Lewis?" she asks.

"I don't know," he says. "Don't you have a watch?"

"I get used to being with Charlie. He always knows the time."

"I wonder if you can hear the bells at the top of the Polish Credit Union Building from here. They chime hours. I can hear them from my bedroom at home."

"I have an electric clock in my bedroom. I don't hear anything until the morning alarm."

Nothing except Mom, and the TV, and the plumbing.

The hole in the vault floor is too small for Charlie's head and shoulders to fit through. He tries the left side, and then the head. Good. Good? Well, good-ish.

He's kneeling on the floor of the tunnel now, with one hand and his head sticking through the hole, and . . . and . . . he can't move any farther. Meanwhile, the stone is cutting into his back. Not so good. He rests a second, tries to work the other shoulder through the hole. Can't. The other arm? He squeezes his other hand up and pushes himself up with his legs. Nothing. There isn't enough room.

Charlie stops in the middle of pushing and lifts his head to the heavens. All his life he's heard that. *Not enough room.* Squeeze in. Scrunch up. Skooch over. Everyone says it. *There isn't much room.* Why isn't there a lot of room? Why can't there, just once, be a lot of room?

And, as if by magic, there is suddenly room. A lot of room. The tightness around his shoulders fades, giving way to a soft and expansive sense. He can spin around with his hands wide. He can stretch out luxuriously, extending his fingers and toes into the comfort of a soft sand-dune world. There is a huge feeling of spaciousness all around him. He can feel the wind in his hair and hear gulls crying. He breathes deeply, inhaling fresh salt air. A wave breaks, and he knows that it has rolled across a third of the world before crashing onto this shore. Ahhhh, space.

He shakes himself all over and takes one last stretch, spreading his arms wide enough to pop the joints in his wrists and elbows. Now he's ready. He hunches over and twists his shoulders around, contorting himself back into reality.

His head, left shoulder, and arm are all inside the vault. His torso, right arm, and legs are in the tunnel. He tries to twist himself through the opening. It's not easy. There's too much resistance in his body. His back still hurts where the bug stung him. He tries to relax. He remembers reading somewhere that muscles take up less room if they are relaxed. If he could find a way for his muscles to relax, maybe he'd be able to squeeze in.

He won't let himself think that he's stuck. He won't let himself think about being trapped in a vault full of dead bodies. He won't!

He tries to distract himself by identifying smells. He used to do this as a little kid, clearing his nose first and then tracking various odors around the apartment. Mom was so embarrassed when he found the half-eaten chocolate bar in the bathroom cupboard. "I don't know how that got there," she said, hurrying to throw it out.

He plays the game now, pinching his nose with his free hand, then taking a deep sniff. There are a lot of smells. Stone, dust, mold, wax, dog . . .

Wait a minute. Wax.

Charlie sniffs again. Yep. It's quite clear. A waxy smell, somewhere between candles and butter. The smell of Mrs. Yodelschmidt's apartment.

Thoughts tumble into his head. Could Underglow be working with Mrs. Yodelschmidt? Charlie tries to remember what Underglow said about his home life. He liked talking about his grandpa, but didn't get along with his dad, for some reason. Something about marrying the wrong woman and rejecting the stapler king. Could the wrong woman have been Mrs. Yodelschmidt?

Is that the link? Is Mrs. Yodelschmidt really Underglow's mother? The thought is so strange, so bizarre, that Charlie lets out a long low whistle.

Do you know what happens when you let out a long low whistle? Try it now. Go on. See? You empty your lungs right out. All the air goes out of your body, and your muscles go slack.

With no air in his lungs, Charlie can slide both shoulders through the hole in the floor.

Ten seconds later he is standing on the floor of the vault, rubbing his aching shoulder, wishing he knew how big the place was. He has to find the money.

A small whiny voice inside him whispers, *How will you get out?*

He ignores it.

No, really, the voice goes on. *It's an awfully tight squeeze through that hole in the floor. What are you going to do if you don't fit?*

He tells the voice to shut up.

Oh, sure, says the voice. *Shoot the messenger. It's not my fault, you know. I'm on your side. For my part, I hope you get out. But you won't!*

The first thing is to determine where the money is. Charlie gets down on his knees and moves forward with his hands spread out in front of him.

It has been exactly thirteen minutes since he entered the tunnel.

Scene 35A: *Flashlight*

Bernadette and Lewis are sitting on a square flat tomb near the entrance to the tunnel when they notice the moving light. Not a beam, but a glow, like headlights coming toward you from behind a hill. This particular headlight is shining from behind the wooden fence at the north end of the cemetery, and it's moving along the fence toward the gap. Bernadette grabs Lewis's arm.

"Someone's coming!" she whispers, sliding off the top of the tomb. PETER GRINDSTONE, it says. He died last year. Lewis jumps down after her. They peek around the corner of the tomb.

The light is through the gap now and bobbing toward them. Flashlight, it must be. Its beam bounces irregularly up and down as the holder moves up the hill.

Lewis is whimpering something about being "the third friend." She tells him to shush.

The beam of light bounces up the hill and stops. The moon is behind a cloud again. Bernadette is behind Grindstone. Lewis is behind Bernadette. The flashlight is in front of the Pater vault. The intruder puts down a briefcase-size something and takes a small something else out of a pants pocket.

What's going on? she wonders. What is this figure doing with the Pater vault? Why Pater and not Underglow? And who is it? Is it Mr. Underglow?

One thing for sure: It's not Mrs. Yodelschmidt.

She sticks her head out from behind the Grindstone tomb to see better. The stranger has the light in the crook of one arm so that both hands are free to deal with the padlocked door. Bernadette can hear the chains banging against the metal framing. Noisy things, chains.

Bernadette has a better view of the mystery figure now. He's a light-skinned guy, not tall or fat. He's about the right size and shape for Underglow. She can't see his hair or face.

He suddenly stops what he's doing and sends the flashlight beam arcing around the graveyard. Bernadette just has time to scuttle behind the tomb again before the beam stabs her. Lewis is pressed against the solid marble slab, trembling like a tuning fork.

Bernadette peeps out a moment later. The man is unwrapping the chains from the vault door. She comes to a decision. She grabs Lewis's arm. "We should call the cops," she says. "It's our best shot. One of us—"

"I'll do it," says Lewis, standing up.

"—should go now," she finishes. "I was going to ask if you'd rather stay, but I guess not."

She gives him her keys. "Phone from my apartment," she says. "Tell them there's . . ."

But Lewis is already gone.

Another mass of cloud swallows the moon, and Bernadette's heart sinks inside her. She is alone in a graveyard in clotted darkness. A mosquito whines nearby. She has to bite her lip to keep from screaming.

Detective Perry sips her coffee tiredly, wondering how much longer she'll have to stay here tonight.

Not much longer, apparently. Madeline Maynard is losing her patience. "Captain Davicki," she snaps. "I'm sorry I agreed to this extended interrogation. You've clearly got nothing to offer my client. As far as I'm concerned, we can adjourn until after the big press conference tomorrow morning. Roger, remember to shave. You can look nervous in front of the cameras, but you mustn't look sloppy."

"Excuse me," a duty officer whispers in Perry's ear.

"What?" She doesn't turn around.

"Culverhouse is on the phone. Says it's urgent."

Hot coffee splashes as Perry leaps to her feet. Culverhouse has been searching the Fairmile apartment all evening. She didn't want to give him the assignment, because he's an idiot, but Davicki insisted. Culverhouse is also the police commissioner's nephew.

Has Culverhouse found something? Who'd have thought it? "Transfer the call to my cell, would you?" she tells the duty officer.

"D'you want a cloth? Coffee'll stain that nice suit."

"No, I'm okay." Perry holds her wet pant leg away from her skin.

Charlie's not okay. He's explored every inch of the vault, and he hasn't found the money. His knees are scraped. His face is covered in cobwebs. He has counted six coffins, stacked in rows like bunk beds. One of the lower-bunk coffins is in poor shape, the handle almost ready to come away from the wood. One of the upper coffins is very small.

He tries not to think of rotting flesh and crumbling bones. He tries not to think about maggots and falling-away faces inside coffin lids. The waxy smell of the bones is bad enough. It's not unpleasant, but it sticks in the back of his throat.

He slumps down on the floor between two rows of coffins. He's worn-out, mentally and physically. His back still stings. He can't think about pawing through the coffins. He can't. Lurking at the bottom of his mind, like a snapping turtle at the bottom of a still pond, is the fear of being trapped. He is not looking forward to squeezing his way back out the hole in the floor.

That's when he hears the rattle behind him. Someone is playing with the lock on the door to the vault. He is momentarily alarmed, and then figures it must be Bernadette.

She and Lewis must be getting worried, after, what, twenty-four minutes now. Poor guys. They don't have a flashlight now. They won't be able to see much more than

The rattling continues. Charlie presses his ear to the other side of the door. He hears something that sounds like chains, rattling and clanking outside. He gulps and moves away. He knows it is stupid, but he cannot help imagining a ghost, carrying the burden of past sins, come to visit the family tomb and punish any intruders.

Rattle. Clank.

Charlie takes another step backward, stumbles over a coffin corner, and falls heavily to the floor behind a stack of coffins. He hears the chains again, and the creak of rusty hinges. The door to the vault is opening. Charlie lies as still as he can on the stone floor. Something is digging into his sore back.

There's light against his eyelids. Instinctively, he ducks lower, behind the coffin. What is he lying on? Something long and thin and hard and knobby. He reaches down.

A bone. A big one—leg bone, maybe. He's holding a human bone in his hand. Charlie puts it down as quietly as he can. The waxy odor is much stronger than it was in the Yodelschmidt apartment, but it's the same odor. Human bones.

Oh, Casey.

Detective Third Grade Culverhouse is clumsy and active—a bad combination. Lucky for him, he's the apple of his auntie Nora's eye, and she's the police commissioner. What's he up to now? Perry wonders. She's having trouble hearing him on her cell phone. Something about a little boy and an emergency.

"Where are you, Culverhouse?"

The line erupts in a succession of sputters and clear patches. Perry tries to piece together what Culverhouse is saying.

". . . met this boy Ellieff in the hall outside . . . strange story . . . with a girl and Fairmile's blind kid . . . in the cemetery." The line clears momentarily. Culverhouse's voice rings out loud and irritating. *"These kids have found the Stocking Bandit's money."*

The effect of his words is electric. Her eyes open wide. She grabs her suit jacket and runs down the hallway. "Hang on to your kid," she cries, holding her phone away from her ear to pull on the jacket. She's in the squad room now. "What'd you say his name was—Ellieff? Hang on to Ellieff. I'm coming, Culverhouse."

The line cuts out again. Detective Perry throws her cell phone in her pocket. "Send a squad car to the Copernicus Street entrance to the Jamestown Cemetery," she calls to the dispatcher. "I'll meet it there in five minutes." She races for the door.

"Ellieff?" The duty sergeant turns to the dispatcher. "Did she say *Ellieff*? I thought Ellieff was a domestic disturbance over on Grant Street."

"Must be a different Ellieff," says the dispatcher.

The intruder speaks, which is weird because he's not speaking to anyone who's there. There's only one set of footsteps, and one voice. Charlie is jolted when he hears the voice. There's pain in it, and anger, and triumph, and something like madness.

"Here we are, Daddy," he says. "Hang on while I unwrap you now."

Charlie hears the chains being put down, then a sound of ripping and tearing, and then a quiet clink, as of someone putting down a vase.

"Don't you look nice here in the middle of the Pater family vault, surrounded by all the other dead Paters. Magnificent!" The intruder laughs.

Charlie is jolted again. He was jolted when he heard and recognized the voice. Not Underglow's. Now he's jolted when he realizes that the tomb he has crawled into is not Underglow's either.

Wrong man, and the wrong place. Did I get anything right? he wonders.

"I chose this vault for the name, Daddy. Yes, my own *paterfamilias,* I thought it was fitting. All the real Paters—the whole family—are dead, just like you. They were rich and now they're dead, and you can join them. You'll have a great time here, surrounded by death and money."

The light flickers across Charlie's eyelids. Footsteps echo to the right and left and right again. The ghost figure is pacing up and down the central aisle of the vault.

"Do you know when it all came together for me, Daddy? Do you? It was after you died, and I was settling your bank account. Yes, I was standing in that little branch bank on Round Valley Road, near your store, when an armored truck pulled up, and they reloaded the cash machine. When I saw the whole front panel swing open, and the stacks of money going in, I knew. I knew what I wanted to do, and how, and why."

The emotion is real, thinks Charlie. This is a real conversation. His daddy may be dead, but he thinks he's still listening.

"The how was easy. I walked down the street to your store, your department, and bought an ax. After all, I was doing this for you. I wanted you to be part of it."

His laugher is full of strangeness. Charlie would be quite frightened, except it's hard to be scared of someone you kind of like, and he kind of likes this man.

"What's going on, Daddy? You're awfully quiet. Getting scared? Not looking forward to an eternity surrounded by dead Paters? Don't be silly. You're going to have a great time, as soon as I find the bags of money. Now, which coffin did I put them in?"

Oh dear, thinks Charlie. I don't like where this is going.

———————

Detective Perry has her foot firmly on the gas pedal. She's doing well over a hundred in a forty zone. Good thing the streets are almost empty at this time of night. She doesn't need the blue bobble light and doesn't want the siren. She makes a skid turn from Grant onto Copernicus. The squad car is parked in front of the Fairmiles' apartment building. Perry stops right behind it and jumps out. The uniformed officer stands beside the driver's side of the squad car with a cell phone at his ear. He nods hello to Perry.

"Is that Culverhouse?" Perry points at the phone. "Are you talking to Culverhouse there?" The officer raises a finger, telling her to hang on a second. He's listening hard. "Does Culverhouse know where to meet us? Does he have the kid?"

The officer nods. He's young, silent, broad-shouldered, very short. The club in his belt hangs almost to his knees. No way he'd have made cop under the old height requirements.

Perry wishes he were bigger, or that he had a partner, but there's no time. She checks her gun to make sure it's loaded. The adrenaline is pumping through her. "Okay," she says.

The uniform puts away the phone, nods once.

An old man is sleeping on a piece of cardboard in the nearby bus shelter. He pokes his head out. "What's going on?" he asks. The uniformed officer waves him back to bed.

Perry takes a deep breath. Zero hour always feels the same. "Let's do it," she says.

In the movies, the music would become scarier as the coffin search gets closer and closer to the hidden hero. But this isn't the movies. Charlie feels the light on his eyes almost at once.

"What's going on?" The light skitters around. The familiar voice is farther away now—he's backed up. "Hey, those dark glasses. I *know* you. Charlie?"

He struggles into a sitting position. "Hi, Mr. Floyd."

"Ayyy, Charlie! Good to see you, man!"

For just a moment, he sounds like the cool teacher. Charlie can hear the smile in his voice. But it is a faint imitation, a hint of his classroom self.

Charlie stands up, keeping the wall at his back and using it for support. "So you're the Stocking Bandit. You've been robbing banks all summer. You . . ." There's a lot he could say, but one thought is uppermost in his mind. "They arrested my dad because of you!"

He doesn't reply. Charlie hears him banging around. "Where's Hugo?" he says. "Which coffin is Hugo's?"

Charlie remembers Mr. Floyd arriving late and flustered, that first day. *There was a holdup,* he said.

Charlie hears a couple of sharp raps with a tool, a sound of splintering wood, and an exclamation of anger from Mr. Floyd.

"I had seven garbage bags of money hidden at the end of Hugo's coffin. One from each bank machine. Now there are only four. Did you take them, Charlie? That's stealing. Stealing from Daddy. And look! Animals have been here!"

Charlie edges along the wall. The door should be to his left. He takes a step. And another. And—

"Oh, no you don't! Get back!" A hard push on his chest. Charlie is unprepared. He falls to the right, scraping his back against the rough stone wall. He hits the floor as the rumbling starts again.

The vault shakes. Charlie, lying on the floor, can feel movement beneath him. He can hear the groan and crash as the building shifts on its foundations and begins to fall in on itself. The floor beneath him is sinking. He breathes dust and starts to cough. The roaring and cracking, the rumbling, are the sounds he and Bernadette and Lewis heard earlier. They're all around him now. A large chunk of something lands on the casket beside him, smashing it to kindling. The wall is giving way behind him.

Mr. Floyd is calling for his daddy. Fainter, much fainter, someone is calling Charlie's own name. He crawls forward, just to be doing something. There is something large on top of him, hindering his movements. He cannot stand.

Charlie feels time slow down. This is strange for him. He's always experienced the passage of time as a constant. Now, focusing inward, he hears the numbers in his head, clicking slower and slower: 10:57:58, 10:57:59, 10:58. Two minutes to eleven. Past his bedtime.

He hears his father telling him not to worry. He hears his mother asking if he's sure. He hears Alf the bus driver telling him to step up. He hears the calm electronic voice of the PAWS screen reader, reminding him to double-click to continue.

He wants to ask PAWS if this particular screen is over, but he can't move his hand to double-click, and he doesn't know how to put his request in words. Oh well, he thinks.

There is a ringing in his ears and a tightness in his throat. And then there isn't.

SCENE 37: *Lucy*

The Pater family vault is in ruins. The process of destruction has been cat-quick: two minutes from start to finish. When part of the floor collapsed onto the tunnel, the nearest wall went with it. That brought the roof down, and another wall. Then the rest of the floor, with most of the coffins. Now a section of the northeast corner—farthest away from the tunnel—is the only part of the memorial still standing. The ridge and hillside of the cemetery are covered in rubble, and money.

The air is full of dust, and money. All twenties. Falling masonry broke open the garbage bags, and the east wind has done the rest. The bills lie in drifts like autumn leaves, swirling and tumbling across the cemetery toward Copernicus Street. Culverhouse and the uniformed police officer are picking through the rubble. Detective Perry is on the phone with Captain Davicki, arranging for emergency services and to reroute traffic. Lewis and Bernadette are back on the Grindstone tomb, out of the way. Lewis, strangely for him, is quiet and withdrawn. Bernadette, strangely for her, is crying her eyes out.

She has never felt worse in her life. Charlie is dead, crushed by falling rubble when the tunnel caved in. Her best friend gone. Her only real friend—you can't count Lewis. What will she tell his parents? What will she do tomorrow with no one to look after? And the next day, and the next. It's worse than when her dad left. Then she had Charlie. Now she has no one. He's dead, and it's all her fault. If she hadn't dropped the flashlight. If she hadn't decided to wait until midnight. If.

She doesn't care about the Stocking Bandit. She doesn't care about the money. She is desolate. That's when she hears the music. A full rich choral sound, like a church choir. The word she hears is *Behold.*

The uniformed officer notices the baby's coffin sitting high on a pile of rubble. Little Lacy Pater, a rich war orphan, died of influenza in 1919. Her aunt Lynn, last of the Paters, bought a lead-lined casket for Lucy and placed it in the family vault before moving to Washington State, where she married a lumber baron and lived happily into the 1960s. The casket is resting on two stone supports, both of which are intact. The officer pulls the casket clear of the surrounding rubble, and there is Charlie's body beneath it, curled up and unharmed. Even the sunglasses are intact. The officer smiles down at the boy, turns, and beckons to Bernadette.

Charlie wakes when he hears the music. He sits up. He is outside, and yet the smell and feel of death and cold stone is all about him. The echoes of the music die quickly in the night air. He knows the music, knows who must be somewhere around.

"Gideon?" he says. Then he's distracted, because he hears Bernadette calling his name over and over. He stands up, shakily.

"Charlie! Charlie!" She runs right into him, almost knocking him over. "Charlie, you're alive!" He smiles. She has her arms around him. She smells like dust and tears. "I thought you were dead," she says. "I thought you were buried under the vault."

"I was inside it. The tunnel went right into the vault," says Charlie. "Only it wasn't the vault I thought it was. It wasn't Underglow's vault."

"Yes, I know." She hugs him again, hard enough to hurt. "I thought you were dead. And then I heard music. You know the music. Say, where is he, anyway?" She breaks away. "It was his music. You know the guy I mean."

"Gideon?" says the police officer, at her elbow.

Bernadette turns. It's Gideon's voice, but it's the police officer speaking. She stares down at him. Hard to tell in the moonlight, and in the uniform . . .

He takes off the cap. Crew cut, impish smile—it's him, all right. "But you can't really be a cop," she whispers. "Can you?"

He winks.

Lewis arrives with the woman detective they know. "So you found him," she says. "Good work, Officer . . . um . . ."

"Gideon," says Gideon.

"Gideon." She frowns, momentarily distracted. "Say, you're not from the Fifty-second Precinct. I don't know you. You must be somewhere uptown, hey?"

"Sure," says Gideon.

For a second—just a second—everyone in the cemetery is silent. And in the sudden and surprising silence comes a sound Bernadette almost never hears from her street: a clock tower ringing the hour. "Eleven o'clock," says Charlie.

"Is that a church tower?" Perry asks.

"Polish Credit Union," says Lewis. "Over on Fern Avenue. I can hear it from my bedroom."

"Detective Perry!" Culverhouse waves his flashlight from the corner of the vault that is still standing. "I think I've killed someone here!"

"Oh, Culverhouse," Perry says under her breath.

"Sorry, Detective Perry—I knocked against this wall, and a piece of it fell off and landed on this guy." He bends over. "Male Caucasian, midforties, dark clothes. He's not in a coffin."

"Don't touch him! I'm coming!" Perry hurries over, Gideon at her heels. Without trying, he seems to move as fast as she does.

"It must be that stranger," says Bernadette.

"Yes, it's Mr. Floyd," says Charlie.

"Really? Mr. Floyd?" Bernadette blinks.

"I talked to him inside. Take me to him now, Bernie. He's the Stocking Bandit."

"*What* did you say?" cries Lewis, shocked out of silence.

"Take me now, Bernie. He may not be dead."

"Can do." She leads him as quickly as she can. It's weird that Mr. Floyd should be the Stocking Bandit, but she doesn't really care. Charlie's alive.

"Mr. Floyd, our *teacher*? Are you sure?" Lewis cares. "He can't be the bandit."

"Hurry," says Charlie.

They do hurry, but they're too late. Culverhouse and Perry stand in front of the body, blocking the way. "Let me talk to him," says Charlie, trying to push past them. "If he confesses, you'll have to let my dad go. Please let me talk to him."

"Sorry, Charlie. You can't."

"It's Detective Perry, isn't it? I recognize your voice. You drove Bernadette and me to the police station. You told me that missing homework was the least of my worries. Do you remember that?"

"Yes, Charlie." She speaks gently.

"Well, I did *your* homework on this case. We did it. Lewis and Bernadette and I. We found the money, and we found the Stocking Bandit. Are you going to let my dad go now?"

She doesn't reply.

"What's wrong? Isn't there any proof? Did Mr. Floyd confess?" Charlie asks.

"He died without saying anything."

Charlie is very tired. He feels around for a clear patch of ground and sits. Bernadette kneels beside him. Lewis, the third friend, stays on his feet.

"Why did it have to be Mr. Floyd?" he moans. "We were going to have the cool teacher all year. Now we'll probably get some weirdo who lives with his mom."

They hear a siren's brief *whoop whoop* as an emergency vehicle runs through an intersection on the red light. Help is on the way.

Perry and Culverhouse are whispering together. "Did I screw up again? I didn't mean to kill the guy. I just leaned against the wall, and . . . well . . ."

"And it fell on him. He might have lived a little longer, might have said something, maybe even confessed—and now he won't." Perry sighs.

"Well, I'm sorry." Culverhouse stares down at Floyd's body. "Do you think this guy here is the bandit? Or is it really Fairmile?"

Perry shrugs. "We'll take this one's fingerprints—maybe there'll be a match on the ax. I don't know. A confession would have helped."

"The blind kid here is Fairmile's, right? D'you know what he did tonight? The girl was telling me about him. He crawled alone in the dark, into a roomful of coffins, to prove his dad's innocence. That's one tough kid." Culverhouse shivers from head to foot.

Perry nods. "I know. You think tough is all muscles and attitude, but it isn't. I don't know too many tough guys who could do what Charlie did tonight."

On the whole, she thinks Roger Fairmile's chances in court would be pretty good, especially with Madeline Maynard as his lawyer. Sure, there'd be a lot of publicity, and people would remember, but he'd probably get off. Probably. Of course, as experience teaches, in court you just never knew.

Charlie's head is bowed. Bernadette is sorry for him. And yet part of her is still hopeful. It's a leftover feeling from before, when she was so sad because she was sure he was dead, and he turned out not to be. Nothing could be as bad as that feeling. She pats him on the shoulder. No one speaks. And, in the utter silence, that feeling pause, Bernadette hears, faint but definite, a sound she almost never notices from her street: a clock tower ringing the hour.

Eleven o'clock.

Bernadette feels as though her mind has been clogged by all the dust she's been breathing. Eleven? Wasn't it eleven o'clock just a few minutes ago?

Detective Perry is looking at her watch. "Hmm. I thought it was later, but I guess it's eleven, all right," she says.

"No, it's eleven-fourteen," says Charlie.

"What do you mean?" says Bernadette. "Didn't you hear the church tower, Charlie?"

"Polish Credit Union. Over on Fern Avenue. I can hear it from my . . . bedroom." Lewis gasps. "Wait a minute. I said that. I'm sure I said that a while ago."

Bernadette stares at him. "This is like the first morning of school," she says. "Remember, Lewis? When Mr. Floyd was taking attendance, and Gideon walked in after the rest of us.

Remember? It was nine o'clock, but Charlie thought it was later."

"It's eleven now," says Culverhouse. "Right now. My watch has a luminous dial, and I set it by the radio every morning when I wake up."

"Eleven-fourteen. Coming up to eleven-fifteen," says Charlie.

"No, no." Culverhouse is frowning. "It's eleven. Mind you, I can't help feeling that . . . somchow . . . I've lived through this moment before."

"Déjà vu," says Gideon.

The three children stare at him.

"It's odd that you should mention that phenomenon," says Perry, "because I was feeling it myself a minute ago. It's wearing off now."

"Hey!" A voice, weak but clear, from the rubble behind them. *"Heyyy!"*

Mr. Floyd is alive.

They stand in a ring, staring down. The flashlights play across the dead man's face. Only he's not dead.

"Mr. Floyd?" says Charlie. "You have to . . . my father is . . . " He drops his cane and holds both hands out in a gesture of supplication. "You have to talk."

He's alive because it's eleven o'clock again, thinks Bernadette. He'll be dead in fourteen minutes, but he's alive now, thanks to whatever Gideon does with time.

She shudders at the idea that he'll be dead again.

"Heyyy, Charlie," he says gently.

One of the flashlights picks up something small and bright-colored lying in the gray rubble nearby. A rubber ball, the kind you find in kids' birthday grab bags. Bernadette frowns at it. Lewis picks it up, puts it in his pocket.

Detective Perry notices that from this angle—downward, with his head to the side—Floyd looks a bit like Roger Fairmile. Something in the line of the jaw. She can see a hint of resemblance. Not much, but maybe it'd be enough to fool a cabbie who wasn't paying attention.

In that moment she comes to believe in Roger's innocence. The coincidence story makes sense now. Floyd took the Steady Cab east along Grant Street from the bank to the cemetery, told the driver to wait, and hid the money in the vault. Enter Roger Fairmile, who sees a waiting cab across the street from his apartment. He gets in and gives the driver the bank address. The driver recognizes the address, doesn't notice the difference in passenger.

Has Charlie ever noticed the similarity between the two men? she wonders. It takes her a second to realize that, of course, he hasn't. For some reason the realization saddens her. She clears her throat and glares around. "We want evidence here. Can you take shorthand notes, Officer Gideon?"

"Sure," says Gideon, pulling out his regulation notebook.

Mr. Floyd takes a long time to finish swallowing. "Daddy's gone," he says. "I dropped him, and he smashed. I should have . . . before. When he died. I wanted to show him. So cheap. I wanted . . . That's how it started. Fantasy."

He takes a rest. He's pacing himself. He wants to talk, Bernadette realizes. To get rid of it. This moment is for him, as much as Charlie.

"Fantasy," he repeats with a smile. "What . . . I didn't do on my summer vacation." He smiles. His shoulders move. He's laughing. Lewis looks horror-struck. Charlie nods his understanding. Bernadette remembers him telling Rachel: *If the truth is boring, change it.*

"Twenty-eight," he says, then frowns and corrects himself. "June . . . twenty-eighth." He swallows again. His throat moves up and down slowly. "Happy Birthday . . . Daddy . . . Northern District Branch," he says distinctly, before taking a long gasping breath.

"Did you get that?" Detective Perry whispers over Gideon's shoulder. "June twenty-eighth at the Northern District Branch was the first cash-machine robbery."

Gideon nods and keeps writing.

Another drawn-out breath. And another. His hand moves.

He begins fumbling at his chest. "Junior," he whispers. "Junior . . . loves . . ." His eyes are closed, his whole being concentrated on his slowly moving hand. Perry shines her flashlight on it, a grotesque thing, bent unnaturally, a cramped claw scuttling across his shirtfront. Bernadette can't bear to look at it. ". . . loves . . . you . . ." He's found what he wanted in his shirt pocket. A black shapeless thing. He holds it in his hand.

"Mommy!" he screams, staring sightlessly into the sky. It's painful to listen. The word is an expression of a great wound and need. The police sergeant shifts uncomfortably. Lewis covers his ears.

"Mommy—look out!" The tendons on his neck stretch like taut cables. Slowly, he raises his arm to point up, maybe at the sky, maybe at his mommy. He opens his hand, and the shapeless thing slides to the ground. Bernadette has never worn one— may never wear one—but she recognizes a black silk stocking when she sees it.

Charlie squeezes her arm, leans toward her. "What'll happen to everyone now?"

CHAPTER FIVE

SCENE 38: *Everyone*

 Miss Callaghan is disappointed. Rising later than usual, she finds that the police have picked up thousands of dollars from the street outside her apartment. "I suppose *you* got some, Desiree," she says to her friend Mrs. Danton. "You usually do."

Detective Perry is busy. She figures to close the file on the Stocking Bandit soon. Officer Gideon's notes are very helpful. She didn't realize how full and clear a confession Junior Floyd was making. He even mentioned buying the padlock and chain for the vault at Solarski Hardware at the same time

as he got the ax. Perry's report makes no reference to Culverhouse's clumsiness.

Alf the bus driver is lying in the Garden Room of the Ma-
coubrey Funeral Home on College Street East. The head of
Infectious Diseases at Mount Sinai Hospital said she'd never
seen blood poisoning spread so fast from a toe to the vital
organs. Visiting hours are from six to eight tonight. Funeral
tomorrow. No flowers by request. "Alf did everything suddenly," says more than one fellow driver.

Uriah is rich.

Titus Underglow III is chagrined. "Imagine how I felt
when I saw my poor gran's name on the television screen. She
cared so much for privacy." He gives Charlie a detective story
to read. "Since you seem to be good at solving mysteries.
However did you come to suspect Mr. Floyd, Charles? I
would as soon have suspected myself." He smiles at the very
idea, wondering why the boy looks somewhat sheepish.

The police commissioner is a beanpole with a long Irish jaw
and iron gray hair worn short. She drinks bourbon, bets on
football, and takes her kids hunting. Just one of the guys.
She's leaning back in a big leather chair, holding a cup of
coffee in her lap, trying to understand. "Let's see if I get it,
Davicki," she says. "The Stocking Bandit is not Roger Fairmile after all. It's a guy named Junior Floyd, who hates his
dad because he—"

"Arthur, Commissioner."

"Huh?"

"His name is Arthur Floyd Junior. His father's name was Arthur, too." Davicki is leaning forward in his leather chair. His coffee is on a coaster on the commissioner's big desk.

"Fine. Now, Junior's dad is too cheap to let Mom take a cab, and she gets run over, and he blames his dad for his mom's death. Right?"

"That's what Perry says."

"Perry? Oh, yes. Detective Perry. I remember her. But let's get back to Junior. Okay, watching your mom die is a horrible thing. Maybe it throws you off-kilter a bit. Okay. So Junior hates his dad. But he doesn't do anything about it. He doesn't break the law or join a gang or take drugs or anything normal. Oh no. He becomes a schoolteacher until his dad dies. *Then* all the anger comes out, and he starts robbing banks."

"Yes, Commissioner."

"Why?" She spins her chair around, puts down her coffee, and slaps her palms on the desk. "I don't get it. Why does robbing bank machines stick it to the old man? Is it the cash? Is it the illegality? Is it the power, smashing the machine? Smashing authority?"

She picks up the coffee again. It's cold, but she drinks it anyway.

Davicki shrugs. "I think he wanted to do it while his dad

was alive, to show him . . . whatever he wanted to show him. But he couldn't. So he waited until he died, and then acted. A fantasy. And his dad *was* cheap, remember. I think he was talking to his dad, saying, *I'll show you, you cheapskate. I'll use your ax to get great bags of cash, and then I'll bury you in it.*"

"Did he use his dad's ax? Did he really? I didn't know that, Davicki. That's interesting. We found the ax, didn't we?"

"Yes, Commissioner. In the cab." Davicki puts on a pair of horn-rims to flip through the notes. "Here we are. The cab-driver found the ax yesterday. Three full matching finger-prints and a partial."

"And could they prove it really was his father's ax?"

"No, ma'am. It was almost new. It almost certainly wasn't his father's actual ax. But the handle of the ax was stamped with the name of the hardware store where his dad worked for eighteen years."

The commissioner frowns. "Not the old man's actual tool."

"No, ma'am. A sort of stand-in. Hell, his father may not even have had an ax."

"Well, well. And then he plans to bury his dad and the cash in an abandoned vault. Funny about the name on the vault, eh? Pater. I remember that one from high school Latin."

"Ironic."

"They don't teach Latin in school anymore, Davicki. I've a

teenager at home wouldn't know a *pater noster* from a baloney sandwich. Ah, well. I wonder how many abandoned vaults there are out there? I suppose families die out, even rich ones. There must be derelict tombs all over the place, waiting to fall down. So, anyway, our man Junior has the fantasy all planned, a way to get rid of his dad, and then this blind kid shows up and skews the whole thing."

"Not quite, Commissioner. The dog shows up, looking for—"

She holds up her hand. "Let's skip that part, if you don't mind. Now Junior's dead. Case closed. Our only worry now is a suit for false arrest by Roger Fairmile and that awful Madeline Maynard."

Edna the cashier is agog. Cherie Lyall's daughter has her picture in the paper. She calls her own daughter over to look. "See, Anastasia? Right at the top: 'Daring Teens Capture Stocking Bandit!' That girl's mom is in here at the Money Mart every month. She tells me all about Bernadette. Says she's getting to be a real handful." Anastasia thinks one of the boys in the picture is kind of hot. Not the skinny one with the shades. She likes the shorter one with the curly hair and glasses.

Frank is self-conscious. He's never stolen flowers before. What if someone sees him, and laughs? He grabs the biggest bunch he can find and runs all the way from the fruit store to the school. He leaves the flowers in front of Bernadette's locker and hurries away.

Gideon is gone. Funny thing, though. Bernadette is sure she's seen him a couple of times. Once she thinks she sees his face on the side of a city bus, but it turns the corner before she can be sure. That night, flicking through the channels, she stops at a fashion show where an ultrafamous model is walking down the runway with—well, with Gideon. He's dressed in slouchy leather and looks pretty silly. But it's him. There's a close-up of him, and the pop sound track changes, just for a second or two, to some kind of churchy music. Gideon winks right into the camera, and her heart lifts.

Mrs. Yodelschmidt is on a last-minute vacation, with Casey, her mink coat, and a bulgy suitcase full of cash.

Bernadette and Charlie are famous. They have told their story a dozen times: to the police, their parents, the police lawyers, Charlie's dad's lawyer, the police again, and then, over and over, to the media. For some reason, everyone loves it that Charlie is blind. They want to get his perspective on things. His special point of view. He says he doesn't have one.

Roger is employed again, as of next week. He gives his son all the credit for his release and plans to frame the magazine picture of him and Charlie shaking hands in front of the police station. With the boy so much in demand these days, he and Gladys often have the apartment to themselves, and they don't mind a bit.

No one is moving to Winnipeg anytime soon.

Bernadette is enjoying her very first limousine ride. The car is movie-star white and almost as big as her bedroom. The TV show they talked to this morning is letting them use it all day. The driver's name is Pierre, and he's from Haiti. He laughs when she and Charlie have bouncing races down the long bench seats. They're on a big street way downtown, somewhere near the train station, when she sees a familiar face.

"Hey, Charlie, there's Monsieur Noël sitting on a bench." She peers through the smoked-glass window. "He looks sick. Stop, Pierre! It's our French teacher. We can give him a lift home."

Pierre is a sweetie. He pulls over, stopping traffic behind them, runs around to let Bernadette and Charlie out, and walks with them to the bench. It's a touristy part of town. The streets are cobblestone, the sidewalks are wide, and the storefronts are very colorful. Theirs is not the only limousine on the block. Monsieur Noël stares at the car, stares at them, and gives a sickly smile. "Well, hi," he says.

She can feel her heart shriveling, drying against her ribs. She wishes she hadn't seen him, hadn't stopped.

Pierre asks him a question in French. He transfers the

sickly smile to the driver. "Well, hi," he says, exactly the way he said it to her.

"Perhaps he does not understand my accent," says Pierre.

"He doesn't speak French," she tells him. "He's not my teacher." She takes a deep breath. "He's my father."

She examines him carefully, running her eyes over the greasy hair, ripped topcoat, scarred knuckles, laceless shoe. His neck has dirt caked into the creases and folds. Will it ever be clean again?

He stares at the double-parked limousine. "Nice." He belches.

"Do you want that we should take him somewhere?" asks Pierre doubtfully. "He's not himself right now."

Pierre is being tactful. "Yes, he is," says Bernadette. "That's exactly who he is."

She takes a step backward. "Bye, Dad," she says.

He blinks. A small frown pecks at the corners of his mouth. "Well, bye."

She stumbles toward the car. Pierre hurries ahead of her to open the door. She's about to climb in when she remembers Charlie. He has tapped his way to the curb and stopped, waiting patiently. She goes back for him, leads him to the car. "Step up, and watch your head," she says. Pierre closes the door after them. Bernadette sits down on the long bench seat and bursts into tears. Charlie tries to put his arm around her, but the car moves forward and she slides away from him, and he ends up punching her lightly in the neck.

"Sorry," he says.

Still sobbing, she takes his hand and places it around her shoulders, and they sit close together in silence and tears, all the way home.

Detective Culverhouse is pleased. For his hard work in tracking down the Stocking Bandit, he is going to be awarded the Police Conduct Medal later this month. "This is great news, Auntie Nora," he says. The police commissioner tells him to stop calling her Auntie Nora.

Lewis is staying with his aunt Mary Lee while his parents try to sort out their differences. Police officers responding to the Ellieff domestic-disturbance call on Friday night found the husband and wife threatening each other with a knife and bowling ball, respectively. Now they are in marriage counseling, and Lewis is sharing a bedroom with his aunt's flatulent bulldog, Winston.

Mr. Sidney Reynolds is bringing his mother breakfast in bed. Mr. Reynolds is the new substitute teacher in Room 24 at Schuyler Colfax Middle School. A no-nonsense pedagogue and traditionalist, he wears zippered cardigans over button-down shirts and believes in parted hair, clean fingernails, and a personal God. His mother, ninety-three years young, is sitting up in her bathrobe, bright-eyed and eager. "It's another beautiful day, dear," he says with a smile as he puts down her tray.

Bernadette squints one Brazil-nut brown eye at the reflection in her cracked bathroom mirror. She is putting on eyeliner for the first time in her life. Looking pretty good, if she says so herself. She's not doing it for Charlie, obviously, or Mom, or anyone else. This is for her.